Kellz Kimberly

D0775926

The Deception of Love 2

Kellz Kimberly

The Deception of Love 2

Chapter 1

Nylah

The last thing I remember is seeing my mother's face; after that, everything went black. I just wanted to get out of there. I couldn't believe that my mom was alive all this time. When I opened my eyes, everyone was standing around me looking at me like I was the person who was supposed to be dead.

"What are y'all looking at me like that for?" I asked them getting up.

"Ny, what happened? I heard you scream, and when I got out here you was passed out" Nick said.

"What happened was that I found out that my mother is no longer dead, she is in fact healthy and well." I said, storming towards the front door.

I couldn't believe I came all the way to Florida for this shit.

"Nylah, wait, what are you talking about." Nick asked, grabbing my arm, stopping me from leaving.

"Nick, what part don't you understand? Your connect, Jay, is my mother, Jazmine. Now, if you don't mind, I am leaving."

I yanked my arm away from him and stormed outside. Diamond came running behind me when it should have been Nick.

"Oh my gosh, Ny, are you okay?" Diamond asked me.

"I really don't want to talk about it, I just wanna get home" I told her.

I was even more pissed because we didn't drive here, we took a fucking cab. As soon as I was about to call a cab, Nick came out of the house with Trey. We hopped in an Audi Q5 and took off. I didn't even question whose car it was cause honestly I didn't care, just as long as I was leaving. The whole car ride was silent, I was sure that everyone was in their own thoughts. As soon as we pulled up to the hotel, I jumped out of the car and went straight to the room. I took off my stuff and just threw everything on the floor and got in the bed.

"Ny, come here," Nick said, walking through the door and sitting at the edge of the bed.

"Did you know?" I asked him.

"Did I know what, Ny?"

"Did you know my mother was alive? Did you know that you was buying your shit from my mother?" I yelled at him.

"Ma, how could I know that she was your mother? I never even seen a picture of your mother."

"But she looks just like me, so how could you not know?"

I felt as though he was lying to me. I didn't know what to believe or who to trust anymore.

"Ma, yes, Jay kind of looks like you now that it is out in the open. But when I was meeting up with her, I wasn't paying attention to that lady's looks. I was just worrying about getting my shit and coming back to you."

He sounded so sincere, a part of me wanted to believe him, but how could I when my own mother deceived me?

"Yea, whatever, tell me anything." I told him.

"It hurts me that you think I would lie to you about this. But I know it's your emotions talking, so I'ma go and chill with Trey. If you need me, just hit my phone. Ight?"

"Okay" I said.

"I love you, Ny"

I couldn't even respond, I just let him walk out the door. I know that I hurt him, but shit, I was hurt. My supposed to be dead mother is my boyfriend's connect.

Nick

Ny questioning me about me knowing about her mother being alive hurt like hell. If I would have known, I would have spoke on it. I didn't know what was going on, but I knew that I had to unwind cause a nigga was stressed. When me and Trey was leaving, Jay told us that Trey's father knew what was going on and have Nylah talk to him if she needs answers. I thought that was strange, but I wanted to know what was going on, so I went up to Trey's room.

"How she doing?" Diamond asked as soon as I walked in the door.

"She's not doing good, but she needs to be alone at least for tonight."

"This shit is crazy" Trey said

"Yea, man, it is, but yo, where your pops at cause I want to know wassup"

"I'm right here, what do you want to know?" Pops said, walking out of the bathroom.

"I want to know everything. My heart is in the next room, crying her eyes out, and asking me did I know that her mother was alive." I said, frustrated to the max.

"Do you know Jay's last name or Nylah's?" Pops asked me.

"Nah, I don't know Jay's last name, but Nylah's last name is Taylor. What does that have to do with anything?" I asked, I had no time for the run around; I just wanted some fucking answers.

"Jay's last name is Royce, and Nylah's last name is indeed Taylor, but her middle name is Royce."

"Wait, Royce, as in the fucking crime family, Royce?" Trey asked..

I'm glad he did cause I was at a loss for words.

"Yes, as in the Royce crime family. Jay gave Nylah a different last name because she didn't want anyone to know that she was part of the family. But she wanted her to carry on the family name, so she gave Nylah, Royce, as her middle name. Jay grew up with a twin sister, who was envious of her. Her sister felt like she should have been the one to take over the family business when their father died, but everything was left to Jay. When Jay first started working in the family business, she met a guy named Knight, who also worked for the Royce family. They fell in love, and a year and a half later, Jay gave birth to her son. Everything was going fine until Jade came back into the picture and slept with Knight. When Jay found out about it, she cut Knight off completely, she still allowed him to see their son, but anything else, as far as a relationship between the two, was deaded. Knight tried to get back on Jay's good side, but she wouldn't let up. Around this time, a war broke out between Jay and the Maxwell family. Jay knew that she had to get her son out of there, so she gave him to a family friend to watch over."

"What does this have to do with Nylah?" I asked; all this back information was real pointless to me right now.

"If you would just sit and be patient, you would find out. Now, since Nick is in such a rush I'ma make a long story short. Two years later, Jay and Knight ended up having another baby. They both felt as though this life was no life for a baby, so Jay opted to leave everything in the hands of Knight. Everything was going as planned, until Knight disappeared around the time Nylah was five. With Jay back in the game, she had to be cautious cause she had a daughter. She already had a family friend taking care of son, how could she ask them to take her daughter, too? So, Jay did what she had to do, she raised Nylah and handled the business. The night that she was in the car accident, her sister was the one that was in the crashed car. Jay put her stuff in Jade's car because she didn't want the police coming to ask questions that she wasn't ready to answer. Jay wanted to come back to Nylah, but I told her that it wouldn't be a good idea, and that it would be better if she went down to Miami, at least until everything died down.

While in Miami, she did some digging, and found out that her sister was helping the Maxwell family. She knew that she couldn't come back because the Maxwell family knew that she wasn't dead, and that it was Jade who was in the car. She stayed down in Miami and only came up to New York to check on Nylah and her son. That is why she asked everyone to come down to Miami, because she wanted to tell y'all the truth about everything." Pops said.

I could tell that there was something that he was leaving out because he was avoiding eye contact.

"So, where was her son at?" I asked him

"Remember how I said that Jay gave Nylah the middle name Royce? She also gave her son that middle name." Pops said.

As soon as he said that, Diamond and I both turned and looked at Trey.

"What y'all looking at me for, just because my middle name is Royce doesn't mean I am her son." He said.

I'm not sure if he knew how stupid he sounded saying that out loud.

"Trey, you are Jay's son." Pops said, looking Trey straight in the eye.

"How can I be her son when I look like you? Her son is by some nigga named Knight." Trey said.

"You look like me because I'm Knight's brother, Jay and Knight gave you to me because you resembled me so much that no one would think that you was Jay's son, which meant no one would come after you."

"Wow, so I'm Ny's big brother, ain't this some shit" Trey said shaking his head.

"This shit is crazy. I don't even know how to tell her this shit." I said, rubbing my hands down my face.

"Since I know how she is feeling, let me tell her. But for now, I just want to go to sleep" Trey said.

Me and Pops got up and said our good byes to Trey

and Diamond, and we went our separate ways. When I got back to the room, Ny was gone. I text and called her, but she wasn't answering. I figured she had got on a plane and went home. I booked a flight for early the next morning, so that me, Trey, and Diamond could fly out together. I sent them a text, letting them now that I booked our flight for tomorrow, and that Ny had left. I then sent Ny a text telling her that I loved her, and that I was here for her, and that I would be back in Brooklyn tomorrow. I was so drained that I just fell on the bed and went to sleep.

Chapter 2

Brielle

I was knocked out from the sex that Jacob and I had a few hours earlier. The only reason why I am up now is because I heard someone banging on my front door. It was five in the morning, and some crazy ass person was knocking on my door. Jacob was long gone, so I got a bat and walked downstairs. I looked out the peep hole, and it was Nylah.

"Nylah, what are you doing banging on my door at this time in the morning?" I asked her, noticing she looked like she just got done getting her ass beat.

She didn't respond, she just walked into my apartment and went straight to my room. I followed her wondering what was going on, I had never seen Nylah like this, other than when she lost her mother. Maybe Nick got killed, I was hoping that was what happened, but I would never let her know that.

"Nylah, what's wrong? You're scaring me; just tell me what's the matter."

"She's alive, she never even died." she said in between sobs.

"Who never died?"

"My mother.....My mother is alive," she said, looking me straight in the eyes.

"What you mean your mother is alive? How in the hell is that possible?" I asked, trying to figure the shit out myself.

"I don't fucking know, Elle, all I know is that I went to go meet Nick's connect, and the connect was my mother. I had to get out of there; I hopped on the plane and came straight here."

"Damn, I'm sorry to hear that, Nylah, but maybe you should talk to her and find out what happened."

"Nah, fuck that, she was alive all this time, and she didn't even try to come see me."

"I understand. What did Nick say about all of this, considering that's his connect, and shit?" I asked her.

"He said he didn't know that she was my mother, but I'm not sure how I'm supposed to believe that when my mother looks like me."

"Damn, I don't even know what to say, but you can stay here as long as you need to." I told her.

"Thanks, Elle, you're the best. I'm gonna take a shower and get out of these clothes."

"Okay, just let me know if you need anything." I told her.

I watched her walk up the stairs and didn't know how to feel. I was happy that in her time of need, she came to me, but damn, I know she's going through it. Like, how do you handle your mother being alive after all this time? I decided I would give Nylah my bedroom, and I would sleep on the couch. As bad as I wanted to be next to her, I knew she need her space.

Nylah

It had been a while since I talked to Nick. It's not that I didn't wanna talk to him; I just wasn't ready to face the fact that my mom was alive. I had been staying with Elle for about three weeks now, and she has been there for me every step of the way. It felt good knowing that I had my best friend there to support me. I had talked to Diamond a couple of times to see how she and the baby was doing. Every time I talked to her, she told me that I should talk to Trey. I found it odd that she was trying to get me to talk to Trey instead of talking to Nick. To say that I missed Nick, was an understatement, I felt like I was going through it without him. I figured that after I handled the Jacob situation, I would go and surprise Nick with a home cooked meal. Me and Jacob have been texting each other ever since I got back, I'm not gonna lie, talking to Jacob felt like we was dating again, and I kind of liked it, but I knew that my heart was with Nick, and I could never trust Jacob again. We agreed to meet up later on tonight, he thought we was going to rekindle what we had in the past, but if he only knew that tonight would be his last night breathing. Elle walked in to the bedroom, followed by Trey, pulling me out of my thoughts.

"Trey came to talk to you." Elle said.

"Ummm okay" I told her.

Trey took off his jacket and sat in the chair that was in the corner. He was about to start talking when noticed that Elle was still in the room.

"I need to talk to her, alone," Trey said, sounding annoyed.

"Nigga, this is my house, unless Nylah tells me to leave, I'm not going anywhere."

I just rolled my eyes at this girl; here she started with that protective shit again.

"Elle, it's cool, if I need you, I will let you know." I told her.

She looked at me with pleading eyes, as if she was begging me to let her stay. I guess when she realized that I wasn't changing my mind, she decided to leave.

"Man, that girl is annoying as fuck." Trey said.

"She can be at times, but what you wanted to talk about. If it is about me avoiding Nick, I already planned on talking to him tomorrow."

"This ain't about Nick, but I'm glad that you plan to hit that nigga up, I'm tired of seeing him looking like he lost his damn best friend."

"If you don't wanna talk about Nick, then what do you want to talk about?" I asked him.

I was confused cause me and Trey never really talked, yea we joked around with each other, but we just was never that close.

"It's about your mother, or should I say, our mother."

"What you mean 'our mother'," I said, interrupting him.

"Ny, calm down, and I mean exactly what I say, our mother......I'm your older brother."

I was in a state of shock when Trey started telling me the story that his father told him. Well, shit, that wasn't even his father, that was his uncle. I couldn't believe this shit, if it wasn't one thing, it was another. Everybody's secrets were coming out, shit, I was scared to talk to anyone else cause I wasn't sure what they were going to tell me. After Trey told me the story, he asked could we go to the mall and just hang out and get to know each other. I agreed to go because I had no right to be mad at Trey, he didn't do anything wrong. Plus, I knew that he shared the same pain I shared, even though his was probably worse than mine. Either way, I wanted to get to know my older brother, I couldn't believe that I even had an older brother. But, I was going to embrace this opportunity; I also planned on talking to my so called mother, because I needed to come to terms with what happened, and the only way that was going to happen was if we talked in person.

Chapter 3

Nick

Ny's ass has been MIA for three weeks. At first, I was blowing her shit up, trying to get her to talk to me about how she was feeling. But after the first week of being ignored, I stopped trying to talk to her. I knew she was all caught up in her feelings, but what the fuck was she ignoring me for? I didn't do shit to her. I knew she was staying at Brielle's house cause she told Diamond, and Diamond told Trey, and Trey, of course, told me. A part of me wanted to go over there and drag her ass out of that house and into my fucking car, but I wasn't gonna let Ny pull me off my square. The games that she was playing was for the birds. When she was ready, she would come to me, until then, I was focused on getting this bread. I had Big still following Jacob, and tonight was the night that we was gonna handle his ass. I was about to go meet up with my niggas, so we could go over the plan, when I got a text from Ny.

My Heart: See you tomorrow daddy, I got a surprise for you so don't make no   plans.

Along with the text, there was a picture attached. Ny was a straight up freak, I sent her a quick text and threw my phone in the passenger seat. Even though I was happy that she hit me up, a nigga still had business to handle. I pulled up to the spot and got out, ready to get this shit over with. When I got inside, all my niggas were dressed in all black with the tims to match. Just looking at us, you could tell that there was gonna be sad singing and flower bringing.

"Ight, look, y'all know why we here, we gonna keep this shit nice and simple. Big said that this nigga just went home about twenty minutes ago, and he had a bitch with him. So, we gonna get in, get our shit, and be out." I said, looking all the men in their eyes.

Everyone nodded their head in agreement, so there was no need to talk anymore. We hopped in the car, ready to handle business. We pulled up on his block and got out of the car. I sent two of my dudes through the back, and me and Trey went through the front. This nigga must have been the stupidest nigga alive, cause when I jiggled his door knob, the shit opened. We checked the front of the house before we went upstairs. Climbing the stairs, we heard moaning, so we knew that we caught him slipping. I slowly pushed his bedroom door open, and what I saw had a nigga seeing red.

Jacob had his faced buried in the pussy, but it wasn't just any pussy, it was MY pussy. There Nylah was, with her legs spread wide open, letting a nigga eat her out. I had to blink a couple of times to make sure my eyes wasn't playing tricks on me, but when I opened them again, Nylah was still there with her legs wide open, but this time she had a gun aimed at Jacob's head. Me and Trey were the only ones upstairs, so I didn't have to worry about anyone questioning why we was just standing there watching instead of busting in the room.

"Jacob," Ny said, sounding serious as hell.

"Damn, ma, what? I was trying to handle my business," he said, bringing his eyes to the barrel of her gun.

"Jacob, you couldn't just leave shit alone, you had to start fucking with his traps and shit."

"Ny, what are you doing? Look at what he has done to you. He turned you into the opposite of who you are. I was just trying to show you the monster that he is." this bitch ass nigga said.

"What the fuck are you talking about? He has not changed me, if anything, he made me better."

"That's not what...." he never got a chance to finish his statement, cause I sent a hot one to his head.

"Ny, get some damn clothes on, and let's go, now." I told her and walked down the steps.

I had to get my mind right, I have seen a lot of shit, but I haven't seen nothing like that. When I got downstairs, my boys already found the stash and had it in the car. I was letting them know everything on me and Trey's end was handled when Ny came down the stairs. All of them just looked at me, waiting for me to explain. But I was the general; I didn't have to explain shit to anyone. Ny said hi to them, and I cut my eyes at her. I don't know why the fuck she was saying hi for, this wasn't no damn social call.

We wiped everything down and was gone within ten minutes. I gave Trey the keys to the car and told him to head back to the trap and make sure everything was accounted for. He didn't trip cause he knew I had to handle shit with Ny. Since Ny drove, I hopped in her car with her. While she drove, I just stared at her. A nigga didn't know whether to feel hurt or honored about the situation. Seeing Ny with her legs open for the enemy hurt like hell, but at the same time, she was gonna end his life for me. I had a ride or die chick on my hands, this the kind of shit that niggas would kill for, so why did I feel so wrong. When she pulled up to the house, I got out and went upstairs to roll a blunt. I needed to just chill and relax before I even tried to address this situation.

"Let me hit that," Ny said, walking into the bedroom. "Here."

I watched her hit the blunt, and that shit looked so sexy.

"Nick, let me explain."

"No need to explain, ma, I know you did what you felt like you had to do. But I never want you to feel like you have get your hands dirty to help me. I got this, ma, ight?"

"Okay, Nick," she said, passing me back my blunt.

"Go get in the shower and wash that nigga off of you, I'ma go home, I'll catch up with you tomorrow." I told her, getting up.

"I love you, Nick." she said, with tears in her eyes.

"Me, too, ma," and I walked out.

I was feeling all fucked up inside. The Ny I saw tonight was not the Ny that I fell in love with. Yea, she was wild as hell, but that is only when you pushed her buttons. The Ny I saw tonight was a completely different person. I couldn't help but hear Jacob's words replay in my head, maybe I did change Ny.

Chapter 4

Diamond

I haven't talked to Ny in a while. Trey put me on to what happened when they went to go handle Jacob. To say I was shocked, would be an understatement. I didn't even know that Ny had that in her. I figured I would go get up with her after I came from my doctor's appointment. I was three months, and I was more than ready to give birth. This whole pregnant thing was not for me at all; I hated feeling needy and shit. The whole time my mom and Trey have been waiting on me hand and foot. It was starting to work my nerves. I had introduced my mom to Trey about two weeks after we came back from Miami, from the way she was acting, you would have thought she was dating Trey. Speaking of Trey, this nigga should have been here an hour ago. I dialed his number to find out where he was cause if he wasn't gonna come pick me up, then I would just drive my damn self.

"Wassup, ma," his deep voice said through the phone.

Just the sound of his voice had my panties wet, Trey's voice was the sexiest voice I ever heard.

"Trey, you know I got my appointment in like an hour, you was supposed to be here already."

"I'm on my way now, I got caught up with some shit."

"Whatever, I'll just drive myself. I don't need this shit." I started to go off on him.

"Diamond, cut it out with that bullshit, I said I got caught up, and I will be there, damn." he said, hanging up.

This nigga had a lot of nerve hanging up on me and trying to put me in my place. He had me fucked up. I decided to call Ny until Trey brought his ass over here cause I really didn't want to drive myself anyway.

"Hey, chick."

"Hey, Diamond," Ny said, her voice sounding all flat.

"What's wrong, mama?"

"Man, what's not wrong? Nick is acting funny as fuck. I think it has to do with that whole Jacob thing."

"He still tripping over that? I thought you said that he understood why you did it."

"That's what he told me the night everything happened, it's been two weeks, and he acts like he doesn't even wanna touch me."

"Damn, Ny, he will come around, and if he doesn't, just remind him what kind of chick he got."

"Diamond, what the hell are you talking about?"

"You need to show him that if he wants to be all caught up in his feelings about some shit that you did for him, then you don't have to put up with it. I know you love him, but you are too pretty to be sitting around crying over a nigga that doesn't know what he's got." I told her.

As soon as I said that, Trey's ass wanted to walk through the door like everything was good.

"You know what, Diamond, your right, I did this crying shit already, and I refuse to do it again."

"That's right, girl, I'm bout to go to my appointment. Let's go to the mall after and find you a new boo."

"Just call me when you leaving, so I can meet you there," she said and hung up.

"Who's trying to get a new boo?" Trey asked, kissing my cheek.

"None of your business, now let's go before I'm late."

"Ma, slow down, the doctors never see you at your appointment time, anyway."

"I'll be in the car, smart ass."

Trey could really work my last nerve, but that was my nigga. I was really starting to fall for him, but I would never let him know it. I always played tough with him, so that I would never let my guard down, especially with me being pregnant right now. I was too vulnerable to get heart broken.

"Why you always acting like that, ma?" Trey asked when he got in the car.

"Why I act like what, Trey? I just want to get to the doctor's, and then, go to the mall and chill with Ny."

"Okay, Diamond, say no more," he said, sounding frustrated.

I know I was pushing him away, but I just didn't want to let my guard down. On top of that, I didn't know how to. I was falling in love with him, and that shit scared me to death. I knew I had to fix my act soon, before he got tired of me acting up, but I didn't know how to let him in. He was my first love, and you know what they say about first loves, your first love is usually your first heart break, and that is something that I wasn't ready for.

Trey

Diamond be on some bullshit, I do everything I am supposed to do as a man, but that shit still ain't enough for her. Shit, her mama treated me better than she did. I wasn't the type of nigga to be doing what I got to do, and get pushed away. If she wanted to push me away, then fine, a nigga wasn't gonna stay where he wasn't wanted. There are plenty of fish in sea, I would always take care of her because she is the mother of my child, but that was as far as this shit was going. If she wanted something more, then she was going to have to work for it.

The doctor's appointment went great, as usual. I was excited about having a baby. I was hoping that it was a girl, I know most dudes want a boy, so they can have a junior, but me, I wanted a little girl. I wanted a girl, so I could show her, her worth and make sure she understood how a female should be treated. Diamond said she was going to meet up with Ny at the mall, so I dropped her off and went to chill with Nick. Ever since Nick caught Ny with Jacob, he has

been drinking and smoking a lot more than what he used to.
My nigga was going through it, for real, for real.

I felt bad for him cause he really felt like he had
changed Ny. I tried to tell him that she had this in her all
along, shit, look at her family history. Shit, our family
history, it was still crazy that she was my sister. Nick said he
was chilling out at the trap in Brownsville, I hated going over
there cause there was always some shit popping off. But, the
chicks were all dimes, so I guess it weighed it's self out.
When I pulled up to the trap, Nick was kicking it with Big
and Q out on the stoop.

"Wassup," I said, giving them all pounds before
sitting down.

"Ain't shit; same shit just a different day." Big said.

"Word," Q said, agreeing.

"My nigga, why you so quiet though?" I asked Nick.

"Just thinking."

"Man, this dude been like this all day, I don't know
what's up with him." Q said.

"Leave my nigga alone, he got his period right now."
Big said, laughing.

Shit, we all laughed at that one.

"Yo, shut the fuck up," Nick said, trying not to laugh.

"Nah, for real though, wassup with you? Why you
acting like you lost your best friend?"

"Man, it's this shit with Ny." Nick said, letting out a
deep breath.

"What? The fact that her mom is your connect is
bothering you?" Q asked.

"Nah, man, when we went to go handle that little
situation, me and Trey go upstairs and find Ny with her legs
cocked open letting the nigga eat her shit."

"Damn!" Big and Q said at the same time, sounding
like Craig and Smoking from Friday.

"Nah, that's not even the best part, before we even
made our move, Ny's ass pulls out a damn gun and points it

at the nigga. When he noticed the gun, they had a little argument, but before she pulled the trigger, I shot him. I couldn't let her kill him."

"My nigga, what are you sitting here looking sad for? You got a thug bitch on your hands. I wish I could find a chick like her. If you don't want her, shit, pass her to me," Big said, serious as hell.

"Aye, nigga, that's my sister you talking bout, chill with that shit." I told him.

"I know, I shouldn't be upset, but that nigga said some shit before he met his maker. He told Ny that I changed her, and that shit got me thinking maybe I did change her."

"Man, you ain't change her, you just brought the shit out of her. Look at who her family is; that shit is in her blood. Don't beat yourself up over this shit, y'all are better than that. You better go get your girl before she get with a nigga like me." Q told him.

"Fuck outta here, Ny would never fuck with your ass." Nick said, laughing.

"Yea, ight, watch, I'm take her from your ass, word, too," Q said.

"Y'all are some fools, you know that." I told them.

We just kicked it for the rest of the day. It felt good just chilling with my niggas for once, with no bullshit. What would be better would be to get into something wet. I text this shawty that I used to fuck with back in the day. She was always down for a good ride, and a good ride was exactly what I needed. She hit me back, saying come through when I was done chilling. If Diamond wanted to push me away, then she could, I wasn't gonna wait around like some bitch, nah, a nigga was too fly for that.

Chapter 5

Nylah

A little shopping was exactly what I needed to get my mind off of Nick. I invited Elle to come with us, she has been such a big help this last month. I was thankful that I had both Diamond and Elle cause without them I didn't know how I would handle this family thing and Nick. They was truly my best friends.

"So when are you gonna go and have a chat with your mom?" Elle asked

"I don't know, I was thinking about going down this weekend" I told them as we got in line at Auntie Anne's.

"You should go, shit, let's all go! We can make it a girls' trip" Diamond said

"Please Trey ain't letting you go anywhere" I told her.

"Trey doesn't control me, the only thing he will have control over is this baby"

"Why act like that when it comes to Trey?" Elle asked.

Diamond just looked at her like she was crazy. Diamond didn't really fuck with Elle, she only dealt with her because she was my friend. We was next in line to order our food. We got our food and sat down on a bench, we continued our conversation when a sexy dark chocolate guy walked up to us. When I say this guy was fine, he was fine, he looked to be about 6'5 and slender; he kind of reminded me of Lance Gross.

"How you doing, ladies," he asked, smiling, showing off the most beautiful pearly whites I have ever seen.

"Hey," we all said at once.

"I was wondering if I could talk to you for a minute." He said, sticking his hand out, so that I could grab it.

22

"You're talking to me." I asked just to play hard to get.

"Yes, you beautiful."

"If I was single, I would take you up on that offer, but since I am spoken for I am gonna have to decline." I told him being polite.

Nick was lucky I wasn't one of them grimy bitches.

"That's too bad to hear, but let me give you my number, just in case you become unspoken for."

I gave him my phone, so that he could put his number in. I had no intentions of calling or texting him. I just didn't want his fine ass to feel rejected. Yea, I was mad at Nick, but I wasn't stupid nor crazy to fuck around on him.

"Here you go, beautiful, if ever become available give me a call. Have a good evening, ladies."

"Bye," we said as he walked away.

"That man was fine. Ny you a good one, because I would have jumped all over that if he gave me the time of day." Diamond said.

"Diamond, sit your pregnant ass down somewhere." I told her.

"Man, listen, I would give him that work." Elle said.

Me and Diamond just looked at her and started dying laughing.

"I don't know what y'all laughing at, but he was fine" she said.

"Come on, I'm ready to go home." I told them.

We hopped in the car, and I dropped both of them off. By the time I got home, I was beyond tired; all I wanted to do was get dicked down and go to sleep. But with the way that Nick was acting, that wasn't happening. The only thing I was getting was an empty bed to sleep in. As soon as I turned the lights on in my living room I damn neared peed my pants.

"Nick, what the fuck are you doing just sitting here in the dark?" I asked him, holding my chest.

"I was waiting for you." he said calmly.

"Waiting for me for what?"

"I wanna talk to you, sit down."

The way he was talking to me was making me nervous. Maybe someone saw me talking to Mr. Sexy. Once again, I talked to a guy and didn't even know his name.

"Okay" I said as I sat down next to him.

"Nylah, you know I love you, right, and I never wanna put you into a situation where you have to change the person that you are. Seeing you with Jacob that night had me seeing red, ma, but when I saw you pull out that gun, I was shocked. Then Jacob said that I changed you, and it had me thinking, maybe I did change you."

"Nick, baby, you didn't change me; I just did what I had to do. I knew that I could get close to Jacob without getting hurt. If something happened to you, I don't know what I would do, so I figured that if I did it, then nothing could possibly happen to you." I told him.

"Ny, that's why I was staying away, it's not because that nigga was eating you out. Yea, that pissed me off, but what killed me was that there could have been a chance that I changed who you were."

"Nick, I love you." I told him, kissing him passionately.

I was feeling all of these different emotions, but I was horny as hell. I took his hand and lead him to the bedroom. When we got upstairs, he laid me down on the bed. The way he looked at me had me a little bit nervous; he was staring at me with so much admiration that I was ready to give him my all. He started to slowly take off my clothes, he was trying to make love, but all I wanted to do was fuck, but I let him run the show. We spent hours exploring each other's bodies, minds, and souls. He took me to a place I have never been before that night. We was both coming when we looked each other in the eye, and said I love you. At that moment, I knew that Nick had me. I was in love, and there was nothing that I could do about it.

Trey

"Yesss! Fuck me, Daddy, just like that," Honey yelled as I had her bent over the couch.

"Throw that ass back for daddy," I told her, slapping her ass.

"Fuck, Trey, I'm coming."

"Fuck, this pussy tight. Damn, ma, I'm bout to come, bend down and catch my shit." I told her.

I pulled out, so that she could bless this mic. Honey was just someone I kicked it with from time to time. She understood our arrangement. She wasn't one of those side chicks that caught feelings and wanted me to leave the one I'm with for her. She had told me from the jump that she was in love with this girl that turned her out a couple years back. I really didn't mind her fucking with a chick because all I wanted from her was a fuck, so I didn't care about her being in love with some bitch. The way she was sucking my dick, you would have thought it was a Popsicle.

"Damn, Honey," I said moaning.

The way she was sucking and making them slurping sounds were driving me crazy. It didn't take long for me to release my shit down her throat.

"Damn, that was good." I told her, sitting back on the couch.

"I know right, you be tearing this shit up," she said, walking off in the direction of the bathroom.

See, that is why I could chill with Honey. She knew when to give a nigga his space, but I could never wife her though. She didn't have anything going for herself. The one thing I hated, was a female that lacked ambition. That's why I was so attracted to Diamond, cause she didn't want a nigga for what he had, cause she had her own. I could see myself settling down with Diamond, but first she need to let that damn wall of hers down. I wasn't Nick, I wasn't gonna keep courting you for you to just push me away, shit, if she wanted me, then she had to let me know, cause if not, I was more than ready to go. I'm not gonna lie though, I felt bad about fucking Honey. I felt like I was doing Diamond dirty, which was crazy cause we wasn't even together. I got up, went in the bathroom to wipe my dick off, and I told Honey I would holla at her later and I left. I wasn't in the mood to be home alone, so I went to Diamond's house. When I got there she was in the bed asleep, so I stripped down to my boxers and just cuddled up next to her and fell asleep. I knew that this is where I wanted to be, but Diamond wasn't ready for what I was offering.

Brielle

I was lonely and bored; my plan to get Nylah had hit a speed bump, so I had to figure out another way to get her. I had been calling Jacob like crazy, but he hasn't been answering my calls. I figured he got out of town cause Nick was looking for his ass. I just hoped he didn't run his mouth about me and him. I decided to call up an old friend and see if she wanted to come over.

"Hello," she said into the phone.

"Bee, wassup"

"Hey, Elle, what you doing up so late?" She asked me.

"Nothing, bored and lonely; you wanna come over?"

"Sure, I'll be over there in like an hour."

"Okay, text me when you're outside." I told her and hung up.

Bee was the first girl that I ever did anything with. I met her a couple of years ago, I knew I liked girls, but I wanted to see what it would be like to have sex with a girl. Since I knew that I couldn't have Nylah, I had to find someone that would let me experiment. I was walking on the board walk in Coney Island when I saw Bee. She was 5'2 and had a honey colored complexion. She had chinky, hazel green eyes and a body to die for. When I walked up to her and started talking to her; the rest of it was history. For a year and a half, Bee was my dirty little secret, but then she started talking about she was in love with me, and that if I didn't love her, then she would tell Nylah everything that I had told her.

After that, I knew I had to get away from her. I told her that I loved her, but I couldn't be in a serious relationship right now until I was able to give her my all. She must have believed me cause for a while she stopped calling me and coming over. About three months back, I ran into her at the mall, and we agreed to catch up with each other. We talked every once in a while since then, but it was nothing major. But I was feeling horny as hell, and she was the only one I knew that would give me what I wanted. I got up and got my room ready for what was going to happen tonight. I didn't want nothing going wrong cause it had been a while since I had sex with a girl. Sex with Jacob was amazing, but sex with a female was something that I couldn't explain. Now Bee was no Nylah, but she would have to do for the time being. Bee text me and told me she was outside. When I opened the door, she was standing there in a trench coat. It was early September, so it was still hot outside.

"Why do you have on a trench coat?"

"Cause I have a surprise under it for you....Don't you wanna see it" she said, walking in my apartment.

"It all depends on what kind of surprise it is." I told her.

She walked into the living room and dropped her trench coat. Underneath it, she had nothing on. She sat on the couch and opened her legs wide, showing me her bald kitty. I envisioned her being Nylah, which had me dripping wet and wanting to devour her. I kneeled down in front of her and took her into my mouth. It was like on contact she was cumming in my mouth, she tasted just like honey. The more she came, the more I wanted.

"Ohh, Nylah, you taste so good."

"Yess, Elle, keeping going," she said, sounding like she could barely breath.

We went at it all night, I know that she herd me call her Nylah, but she didn't say anything. Before, when I would do it, she would go off, but she didn't say anything this time, which made me a little bit nervous. Not nervous as in I was scared, but nervous as in I didn't think that I could trust her.

Chapter 6

Diamond

This nigga must have thought I was stupid. He's not my man, so I really didn't care about him coming to my house all late. But what pissed me off was the fact he had the nerve to get in my bed and cuddle with me while he was smelling like the next bitch. I know we are not together, like we should be, but that is disrespectful. When I woke up, I pushed his ass away from me and went into the living room to watch TV. I wasn't in the mood to talk or argue with Trey, I just wanted to chill and relax. School had already started, and I wasn't ready for that at all. Ny told me that I should take this year off, but I didn't want to do that. School was important to me, getting a degree was my biggest goal, and just because I was pregnant didn't mean I still couldn't achieve my goal.

I had to pick Ny up in about to two hours, so we could go to class. We were both majoring in business, so we mainly had all the same classes. Since I had two hours to kill, I decided to watch Maury. I couldn't believe females on this show; they would go on there and act a fool all for a free DNA test. There is not enough money in the world to make me go on a show like that. For all of that drama, I would just go to a hospital and pay for the test my damn self. I was dying laughing at this girl who swore that a dude and his best friend were the daddies to her two kids when Trey came in the living room.

"Ma, why you laughing so hard? I can hear you all the way up stairs." He said, sitting down next to me.

"I'm laughing because females be grimy"

"I know that's right, they always hollering how a nigga ain't shit but be fucking him and his mans." Trey said shaking his head.

"Your one to talk." I told him.

"Ma, what you talking about now?"

"Let me ask you a question."

"Go ahead."

"Where were you last night?"

"With a chick named Honey." This nigga said, like there was nothing wrong.

He was bold as fuck, but he kept it 100, so how could I be mad.

"Correct, so let me ask you another question."

"Diamond, I'm not trying to play 21 questions, just say what you have to say."

"Ok. We are not together, so I don't give a fuck about you sleeping with the next bitch. I expected you to do that since I'm not giving you any. However, being that I am the mother of your child, you will respect me. Don't you ever, and I mean ever, come into my house and get in my bed smelling like another bitch." I told him.

I didn't even wait for him to respond. I got up went into my bedroom got dressed and was out the door without even saying bye to him. I don't know who this nigga thought he was, but he was fucking with the wrong one. The only thing I needed from him is to do his part when the baby gets here, other than that, I am done.

Trey

Damn. Was the only thing that I could say, I didn't even know I came in smelling like the bitch. I had to fix this shit with Diamond. I called her mother to see if she wanted to go to lunch with me, I need to find out why Diamond was so stubborn and didn't want to be with me. I know I fucked up in the beginning by not being there when she needed me, but I did more than make up for that. For a minute, it seemed like me and Diamond had something going, but the further along she got in her pregnancy, the further she was pushing away from me. Her mom agreed to meet me TGI Fridays for lunch. I started to get ready when my phone started ringing. I didn't recognize the number but decide to answer it anyway.

"Yo"

"Is that how you answer your phone when your mother calls?"

"My bad, Jay...How you doing?"

I wasn't comfortable with calling her mom because I didn't even know her. When I first met her, she was my connect, so to go from connect to mom was hard.

"It's alright, I was calling because I wanted to let you know that I'm in town, and I want to go out to dinner with you and Nylah."

"That's fine with me. I'm free tonight, I'll hit up Ny and see if she wanna go."

"Okay, well then, just call me," she said and hung up.

Shit has just been weird between us lately, me and Ny was getting along cool, I was getting to my sister and everything was going smooth. But Jay, there was just something a little bit off about her. Yea, I felt some type of way about me not knowing my mother, and the guy who raised me not being my real father. That could have been the reason I felt the way I did, I just shrugged it off and hopped in my Benz s550. This car was crack, and it was definitely my baby. I didn't let anyone drive this car besides me. When I pulled up to TGI Friday's, her mom was already there and had been seated already.

"Hey, Ms. April," I said, giving her a kiss on her cheek.

"How you doing, baby.?

"I'm doing ight just trying to live and maintain."

We looked over our menus and ordered our food. Diamond was the spitting image of her mother. Ms. April just looked to be 10 years older than Diamond; she could have passed as her older sister.

"What's wrong, honey? I can see them wheels turning in your head all the way from over here."

"Nothing really. It's just that Diamond keeps pushing me away, and I don't know why. I do everything I can to show her that I care, but she just gives me nothing but attitude." I told her.

"Don't take it personal. Diamond doesn't let anyone get close to her, and I am to blame for that. Growing up, I used to always tell Diamond never let a man get close to your heart, or he will leave you heart broken and lonely. I only told her that because I was lonely, heart broken and bitter. Her father left me a year after she was born. He said that we just wasn't working anymore, but the truth was he had another family. That bastard was married with 4 kids, I was so hurt and angry that I use to make Diamond promise she would never be so stupid and fall in love. I know that was a horrible thing to teach a child, but you have to understand where I was coming from." She said, as she tried to hold back tears.

I understood how she felt, but that was crazy. How could you teach your daughter something that could affect her whole life?

"I understand, I can't say I know where you are coming from because I don't, but I do know what it feels like to be betrayed. I just found out that the guy who raised me is not my father, my connect is my mother, and me and Ny are brother and sister." I said, shaking my head at all that drama.

"Wow that is a mouth full isn't it" She said.

By now our waitress brought us our food and drinks. The conversation while we ate was a little bit tense. I could see that she was hurt that she caused her daughter to be so cold hearted. Shit, I was pissed off at her for the things that she had taught her daughter. But I knew I had to be the one to break down everything and show her that not all love is bad. We finished our lunch and said our good byes. I called Diamond, but it went straight to voice mail. So, I called Ny to see if she wanted to go to dinner.

"Wassup big bro," she said into the phone.

"Nothing, just chilling, yo is Diamond with you?"

"Yea, she right here, we just got done with class, and we bout to head over to my house."

"Ight I'ma meet y'all over there."

"Cool, Nick should be there to let you in," she said before she hung up.

I started my car and headed over to Ny's house. Hopefully I beat them there cause I needed to talk to Nick about this Diamond situation. I had no idea how I was gonna fix this shit, but I knew I had to fix it before my baby was born.

Nylah

"Why you doing my brother like that?" I asked Diamond as we walked to her car.

"Man, please, he came in last night smelling like another bitch and had the nerve to cuddle up against me."

"That's straight disrespect, but I mean, him fucking another chick ain't nothing cause from what you say y'all are not even together." I told her.

Yea, the fact that Trey got in to bed with her smelling like another woman was disrespectful, but that is the only thing that she could have been mad at.

"I don't care about him fucking another bitch cause like I said we not together."

"Diamond what is wrong? You are having that man's baby. Why are you pushing him away like he is the plague?"

"Cause I love him. Growing up, my mom always told me to never be stupid and fall in love. So, my boyfriends never lasted. I would give them their walking papers before shit got too serious. But with Trey, it's different. I love him; I want nothing more than to be with him, to be a family with him. But I have seen what love can do to a person. Shit, I had to watch my mother go through it, and what she went through is not something that I want for myself."

"I understand where you're coming from, but just because your mom had a bad experience with love doesn't mean you will. Don't use your mom's experience as a way to not experience stuff for yourself. Yes, love hurts, but it can also bring you joy. If you love Trey, you need to let him know, don't be scared, just take it one day at a time."

"I don't know, Ny. I'll think about it. Wait, how are you so pro love, when you was just pissed off with Nick."

"Gurrrllll, that nigga was in my living room waiting for me when I came in last night. He started telling me how he loved me, and how he felt like he was changing me, and a whole bunch of other stuff. Then he took me to the room and........."

"Okay, Okay, I get it, you don't have to go any further," she said, laughing at me.

"Whatever girl, last night was amazing. I feel like we are on a good start to getting back to where we used to be." I told her.

We pulled up to my apartment, and Diamond wouldn't get out the car.

"Diamond, you have to put on your big girl panties and handle your B.I. Now let's go." I told her.

She got out of the car and started walking slowly, so I pulled her along. When we walked in, Trey and Nick were in the living room playing Call of Duty on the Xbox One.

"Hey baby....Wassup Bro," I said, greeting them.

I walked over, gave Nick a kiss on the cheek and gave Trey a hug.

"Hey y'all," Diamond said her voice sounding flat.

"Don't mind her, she just tried from class." I said, giving Diamond the side eye.

"Ayo, Ny, your mother called, and said she wanted to have dinner with us, you wanna go?" Trey said.

"She's in town? I was gonna go down there this weekend, but her being here saves me a trip. I don't feel like going out, but she can just come here." I said.

I needed the support of everyone in this room to deal with my mother.

"Ight, I'm going call her right now." Trey said, leaving the living room and going upstairs.

I looked at Diamond, letting her know that this was her time to go and talk to Trey. I guess she didn't catch the hint cause she did not budge from where she was sitting.

"Diamond, don't you have to go and talk to Trey?"

"Ny, not right now"

"Diamond, now is as good of time as any. Now, go upstairs and talk." I told her.

She got up, stuck her tongue out at me and went upstairs. That girl was stubborn as hell. She was the one that was pregnant, but I felt like I was raising a child.

"What was all that about?" Nick asked, walking in the kitchen.

"It wasn't anything." I said, kissing him, and then, nibbling on his neck

"Ny, don't start, ma. We have guests, so don't start something that you can't finish"

"Trey is family, and so is Diamond, so they are not guests, and it's not like we didn't have sex with them in the house before." I told him laughing.

"Ma, you crazy, but get to cooking, your man is hungry." He said, and went back into the living room.

I just looked at him and smiled. He was truly who I wanted to be with. I would do anything for that man of mine. Trey sent a text saying that our mother would be here around 9. I didn't get mad that he sent at text instead of coming downstairs, because I knew that he and Diamond had a lot to talk about. I was glad that everything was at least trying to fall into place. I started to get everything ready for tonight, tonight was either going to make or break our family. I wasn't prepared to face my mother, but I figured now was as a good time as any, and if stuff got out of hand, I could always tell her to leave.

Diamond

I wasn't ready to have this conversation with Trey. But like Nylah said, I had to put on my big girl panties and do what I had to do. Yea, I played hard like Trey fucking other girls didn't bother me, but that shit hurt. I wanted Trey, but I didn't wanna go through the same things that my mom went through. She always told me that when you fall in love, you get hurt in the end. Since my father left, my mom has been bitter and never dated again. I don't want to end up like her. I went to turn around and go back downstairs when Trey called me.

"Diamond, what are you doing standing there like that?"

"Uh, nothing, I came up here to make sure you was cool." I said, trying to think of a lie fast enough.

"Stop lying, ma, Ny already sent me a text saying that you wanted to talk to me."

"That bitch," I said, walking in the room and sitting next to Trey.

He placed his hand on my stomach and started rubbing it.

"Damn, I can't believe I'm gonna be a father in six months." Trey said, admiring my little baby bump.

"I know right, I still can't believe it. This was really unexpected. But I wouldn't change it for the world." I said, looking at my stomach.

This pregnancy was kicking my ass, but I still wouldn't change it for the world. To know that you have a life growing inside of you is something precious.

"You wouldn't even change our relationship?" Trey

asked, looking me in the eye.

"There's a lot I would change about our relationship, like for one, we would be in an actual relationship. I have some issues. Growing up, my mom instilled some things in me that makes me run from serious relationships." I said, looking down, trying to hold back the tears.

"Ma, lift your head up. You don't have to look down when you're talking to me. If you need to cry, then let it go, baby. I know why you run from serious relationships, your mom told me. But what your father did to her is something that I would never do to you. You and this baby are my family. It's just y'all. But you have to let me know how you're feeling and stop pushing me away. Cause I'm gonna tell you now, you keep pushing, and I'm really gonna leave. I will always be there for my kid and make sure you straight, but other than that, I'm gone. I don't play games, so I don't expect you to either."

I heard everything he said. I believed him when he said he wouldn't hurt me, but anything can happen. It was either now or never, and I had a baby on the way, so I at least owed it to the baby to try and see if me and Trey could work.

"I love you, Trey."

"Don't say shit you don't mean, ma."

"I mean it, Trey, I love you."

He leaned forward and started to kiss me and play with my clit.

"Trey, stop we can't do this in their house."

"Shhhhh, we ain't doing nothing, just let me please you."

He push me back on the bed and started planting kisses down my midsection. When he got to my love nest, he started feasting on my kitty like it was the last meal. I was trying my hardest not to scream, but the way Trey was going at it wasn't making it easy.

"Ahhhhh,Trey, yes, I'm coming"

And coming I was. I came all over his face, and he

licked it up like a champ. He went into the bath room, leaving me to catch my breath. When he came back out, he cleaned me up and fixed my clothes.

Right before we left the room, he turned towards me and said, "I love you, too, Diamond."

I smiled. Maybe this could be the start of something new. Only time would tell, but for now, I was going to live in the moment.

Jay

I was glad that Trey and Nylah agreed to have dinner with me. I really wanted to be a part of their lives, but I still had to be careful. I knew that the Maxwell family was gunning for me and would touch anything and everyone I got close to. They had sent a couple of their goons to mimic, but me and my people handled that shit. Without Jade, they were like lost puppies, so I knew I didn't have to worry too much. But I was always told to never underestimate your enemy, so I wasn't sleeping on them. I was a little bit nervous about having dinner with them. I pulled up to my old house that I used to share with Nylah. A wave of emotions came over me when I got out of the car and had to knock on the door. I had to get myself together; this was supposed to be a happy time. After about two minutes of knocking, Nick came and finally opened the door.

"Hey, Jay, come on in." He said, kissing my cheek.

I walked in and everything still looked the same. Nylah didn't change anything about the place besides adding a few new things here and there.

"Where is everyone?" I asked as I took a seat in the kitchen.

"They up stairs getting ready. They will be down in a minute"

Nick started setting the table for everyone. I got up to

help him, but he said there was no need cause I was a guest. After the table was set, everyone came downstairs.

"Hey, Jay," Diamond said first taking a seat at the other side of the table.

"Hi, Diamond, right?" I asked, not sure if I remembered her name.

"Yea, it's Diamond," she answered with a slight attitude in her voice.

"Wassup Jay," Trey said, kissing me on the cheek and then going to sit next to Diamond.

"Hey, Trey."

Nylah walked in and sat next to Nick. I understood she was upset, but her not talking after she invited me here made no sense. Everybody started grabbing bowels and putting food on their plate.

"So, Trey told me what happened," Nylah said, not looking away from her food.

"Look Nylah, I know there is no excuse for the reason why I had to leave you. But you have to understand it was for you own good. I was trying to protect you." I told her.

"Ma, there is no need to explain. I understand why you didn't. But I also want you to know that it is going to take time to get back to where I used to be. I just can't pick up where we left off, I need time."

"Nylah, take all the time in the world." I was just glad that she was being understanding and giving me a chance.

"Trey, I hope that you will give me a chance, also, to make up for missing out on the majority of your life."

"It's okay. Just like Ny, I understand why you did it. I just want a chance to get to know you, and give you a chance to get to know your grandchild."

"Oh my gosh, Diamond, your pregnant?"

"Yes, ma'am, I am 3 months."

"Pregnancy is a beautiful thing. I promise I will be there for both my children and my grandchild from now on."

For the rest of the night we just enjoyed each other

company. This is how it was supposed to be. I wish that we could have had a chance to experience this moment sooner. But regardless of the timing I was glad that it happened. I was also going to make sure that no one ever caused me to leave my family because it's all we got in the end.

We was all sitting in the living room watching some movie that Nylah had put on. I need to talk to Nick and Trey about the Maxwell family, so I asked them could we talk in private.

"Wassup Jay, what you need to talk to us about?" Nick asked.

"I need to put y'all on to the Maxwell family. Now, they haven't been an issue lately, but that can be because their only inside leak was Jade. But that doesn't mean we are going to sleep on them. Make sure you keep your eyes open. If y'all notice anything strange happening, let me know." I told them

"Jay, chill; we not new to this, we are true to this. Ny is my heart, so you already know I'm not gonna let anything happen to her. Trey is my mans, 100 grand, so you know I already got his back." Nick said.

"Yea, Jay, we got this, don't worry." Trey said, getting up to give me a hug.

"Well, I'm bout to go. I have a flight to catch."

They walked me upstairs, and they all said their good byes. When I got home, I went straight up stairs to get in the shower. I was beyond tired, but before I could relax, I had to make a phone call.

"I just got back. Everything is everything," I said to the person on the other side of the phone.

I didn't wait for them to reply back, I just hung up. I got in the shower so that I could enjoy the rest of my night. Cause there was a storm brewing, and when it hit, it was going to hit hard.

Chapter 7

Fast Forward 3 months...

Nylah

It was the middle of the winter and everything had been going great. Me and Nick were still hanging in there and had even moved in together. We got a town house over on the upper east side. It was beautiful. Everyday me and Nick was together, I fell deeper and deeper in love with him. He was like a breath of fresh air. He never stayed out late because of work, and he always checked up on me to make sure I was doing what I had to do in school. That's why I had planned something special for his birthday that was coming up. His birthday was the 3rd of January, so I had about two weeks to get everything ready. I called Elle earlier to see if she wanted to look at venues with me and do a little Christmas shopping. She said that she needed me to pick up her cause her car was in the shop. When I pulled up to her house, there was a short honey complexioned girl leaving. I blew my horn, so that Elle would know that I was there. The short girl looked my way and rolled her eyes, I didn't know what her problem was, but I damn sure was about to solve it for her.

"Is everything okay with your eyes, mama?" I asked, stepping out of the car.

"Nah, there's nothing wrong with my eyes. I was just leaving. Bye, Elle," she said in a seductive tone.

Elle didn't reply, she just got in my car and told me to come on. I got in the car and went to the first venue. I wanted to rent out something that was big and had different floors, so that I could host different things on each floor. So, we went straight to Webster Hall. The guy showed us around and said that it was going to be 100 grand to rent out all three floors. I told him I would take it and put a down payment it on it. The whole time I could tell that Elle was a little salty, lately it seemed like she just didn't wanna be bothered with me. I wasn't one to beg for friends, but if you didn't wanna be my friend, then what the fuck are you around me for? I was gonna figure out what was up with Elle, but first, I wanted to shop. I was tired of shopping at King's Plaza, so I decided to go to Queens' Center Mall.

"Wait, where we going, I thought we was going to KP." Elle said.

"Nah, I wanted to go to Queen Center Mall."

"Hmph."

"What is that supposed to mean?" I asked Elle.

"Nothing."

"Nah, what you mean nothing? You have been acting salty for a minute now."

"You wanna know what my problem is? I am so tired of you thinking that the sun and the moon raises and sets on your ass."

I was at a loss for words because I had no idea where this was coming from.

"Elle, what, the fuck, are you talking about?"

"I'm talking about how you want everyone to kiss your ass, and how your happiness trumps everyone else." she said.

"My happiness trumps who's, Elle? If your gonna state shit at least state facts."

"That's how true it is. You can't even see that you don't give a fuck about me being happy."

"Elle, I do care whether your happy or not."

"Ny, if you cared, you wouldn't rub your fucking relationship in my face. Everything is Nick this and Nick that. You even worry about Diamond more than you worry about me."

"Elle, you bugging, let's end the convo here before

someone says something that they are going to regret."

"No, we are going to talk about this now. Everyone loves Nylah. Your own mother even faked her death to protect you. Even a nigga that you wouldn't give the time of day to dropped me once you started texting him."

As soon as she said that, a red light went off in my head. I knew she wasn't talking about Jacob.

"I know you are not saying what I think you are saying. You was fucking with Jacob?" I screamed, stopping my car in the middle of traffic.

"I wasn't fucking with him, I was fucking him, and as soon as he thought you was back in his life, he dropped me like a hot potato. The nigga won't even answer my phone calls because of you."

"Elle, Jacob is fucking dead, and I can't believe you slept with him. How could you do that to me?"

I was seeing red, whether I wanted to be with Jacob or not, that was my first love, and Elle crossed a line that shouldn't have been crossed.

"I did it for you. I had to sleep with Jacob, so that he could get rid of Nick, so you could see that he is bad for you. I wanted to show you that Nick is no better than Jacob, and that I deserve to have you."

"Elle, what, the fuck, don't you understand? Me and you will never be together. Shit, after this, you would be lucky if I even talked to you after this shit."

By now there were cars honking their horns, trying to get me to move out of the way. I started driving again. I busted a u turn, so that I could go back home. After this shit, I didn't even want to shop again.

"Nylah Royce, I am going to tell you this once, and this once only, if you cannot love and be with me, then I will not allow for you to be with anyone else." She said so calmly.

I didn't even reply. I just drove faster, so that I could get her the fuck out of my car. This was the final straw. I loved Elle like a best friend, but I couldn't take this anymore. My mom used to always say to keep my grass cut, so I could spot a snake. But I didn't think the snake was in my own fucking camp. I pulled up to Elle's house, and she hopped out of the car. She didn't say bye or anything; she just got out and went inside. I didn't feel like hearing Nick say I told you so, so I was going to keep this one to myself. I figured that I would try to go shopping again tomorrow, but for now I was gonna go home and start dinner.

Brielle

Today was the last day I was going to put up with Nylah's shit. If she didn't wanna love me the way that I loved her, then fine, but I would be damned if she'd love someone else. Everyone was going to pay for this; Nylah, Nick, Trey, and Diamond. I wanted them all to pay. I now knew why Jacob wasn't answering my phone calls. It kind of hurt me that he was dead. Yea, I was just using him, but I was going to miss the amazing sex. I wanted everyone to pay for the pain that I was feeling. I didn't care if they caused it or not. Everyone was going to feel my wrath, and Nick was the first one on my list. I had a trick up my sleeve for him. I needed to wind down and find someone that would help me with my plan. I had only three weeks to get this plan in motion, so I had to find someone and find someone fast. My phone started ringing, pulling me out of my thoughts.

"Hello," I said with an attitude.

"So, you didn't have a good date with your, boo?" Bee asked.

"That's not my boo, I'm over that bitch."

"Oh, we calling her names now, are we?" she said.

"I can call her whatever the fuck I want to. I'm tired of kissing her ass while she took me for granted."

"Now, you see why I don't like that bitch. You need a

chick like me on your team, mama."

At that moment, I had the perfect plan, and I knew exactly who was going to help me.

"Your right, I should have just stuck with you from the beginning. You have always been there for me when I needed you." I said trying to butter her up.

"You know you have a lot of making up to do, right? I'm just not gonna come running back to you." She said, trying to play hard to get.

"I know baby, and I will make it up to you. I just need you to do one little favor for me, and then, I am all yours."

"What is it?"

I told her my plan to destroy Nylah and everyone around her. She agreed to help me, but I had to show that I was serious about our relationship. I had no problem making her feel like she was wanted. Cause in the end, I was going to have the last laugh. There was nothing better than two people working together because they had a common interest, and our common interest was to destroy Nylah.

Diamond

Me and Trey planned to have Christmas at Trey's house since Nylah and Nick had Thanksgiving at their house. Everything seemed to be going good between us. I stopped pushing him away, and I was the happiest I had ever been. On top of that, we found out that we was having a girl. I was happy, but Trey was excited. Between him and Ny, I didn't know who was happier. This baby already had more than enough clothes and toys, and she wasn't due for another three months.

"Ma, you ready? I wanna pick up this stuff before everything is gone." Trey said, coming down the stairs.

"Yea, I'm ready, let's go."

We had to go to the supermarket to pick up the rest of

the stuff for Christmas. Even though Christmas was weeks away, I wanted to get everything now, so that, I didn't have to run out last minute. While in the car, Trey was bumping that gangsta shit. I was not in the mood for that, so I put in Trey Songz' new album "Trigga" and went straight to my favorite song.

"Oh man, why do you listen to this shit? This song is all sad and depressing and shit." he said.

"First of all, this song is not shit. It is called Y.A.S. and this is my favorite song." I told him.

"Yea, whatever, man." he said.

My favorite part came up, and I began to sing my heart out.

"Half the man that you think you are, no you ain't. Nothing like all the songs you sing, I hope you change. No better than my ex, other than the sex that I'm never will forget but it's on to the next. And I know you gonna regret when I'm gone, nigga yes. You ain't even took me shopping yet"

I sang that part like my life depended on it. I was about to sing the next part when Trey cut me off.

"Hold up, you saying I ain't shit? Would you even be here with me here, yeah, if I wasn't rich? We can talk about your ex cause you were cheating on him with me. And we can talk about the sex cause that's all it'll ever be. And you know that I ain't talk girl, on you. You're not a good girl, but you try hard to be." Trey sang.

He could really blow just like Trey Songz.

"You was just bitching about the song, now you over here singing it." I said.

"Yea, I couldn't let you tell me that I ain't shit without defending myself." He said laughing.

"I didn't even know you could sing."

"Yea, I sing a little, but I really don't put it out there cause it's just something that I do every now and then."

The rest of the way to the supermarket we just chilled

and sang together. Getting out of the car, I felt like someone was watching us. I turned back to see if I saw anyone, but I saw nothing. Trey was going up and down the aisles, gliding on the shopping cart. I swear he was a big ass kid.

"Trey, stop playing and come on, I'm ready to go home, I'm tired."

"Ma, we just got here, and you ain't even doing anything to be tired."

"Whatever, just come on."

I went to walk into the next aisle, and the first thing I see is Elle. Nylah told me what happened between the two. But she didn't want Nick to know, so I couldn't show out in front of Trey without him asking what was up. I tried to just walk past her, but she just had to open her mouth.

"Females act like they can't say hi to anyone." She said.

"When I see a female then I will say hi. I don't talk to snakes." I told her and kept walking.

Trey was just looking at the both of us wondering what was going on.

"I may be a snake, but just remember, revenge is best served cold." She said, walking away.

I didn't know what that bitch meant by that, but I was hoping that this bitch didn't try anything stupid.

"What was that about?" Trey asked.

"Nothing, don't worry about it," I told him.

He just shook his head. After shopping, he dropped me off and told me that he had a meeting to go to with Nick. As soon as I got in the house, I called Nylah to put her on.

"I saw your friend today," I told her, as I put the food away.

"Bitch, I don't have any friends, and unless you looked at yourself in the mirror, I don't know who you're talking about."

"I saw Elle at the supermarket when I was with Trey."

"Umph, what happened?"

"Well, I tried to walk past her, but she wanted to get slick with her mouth, so I put her in her place."

I left out the part about the revenge because I didn't want Ny to get all upset.

"I don't got time to play Elle's game. After she told me what she told me, I wash my hands clean of her."

"I hear that, I don't know how she could be so fucking sneaky." I said.

The fact that she was fucking Jacob pissed me off, especially since she was supposed to be Ny's best friend. We made idle chit chat about the baby before we got off the phone. I was tired, so I decided to get a quick nap before I had to cook dinner.

Nick

I called a meeting for me and my crew. I need to let them know that even though everything was going good, we couldn't sleep because someone was always going to try and get the crown. When I pulled up to the spot, everyone was already there. That's what I loved about my crew, when there was meeting, these niggas were always on time, and when there was shit to handle, they was always ready to go to war. I walked in and said wassup to everybody before starting the meeting.

"I called this meeting to let everyone know that everything is going smoothly. There has been no shortage of money and no late payments. However, even though everything is going good right now doesn't mean that it will stay this away. As y'all already know, there is always a nigga that is trying to come up. We have to make sure that we are on point at all times." I told them.

Trey looked at me, letting me know that he had something to say, so I stood down so he could address the crew.

"As Nick said there is always gonna be a nigga trying to come up. That's why we are gonna switch it up a bit. If we keep the same routine, niggas will start to catch on, and that's not what we need right now. Starting next week, everything is about to go in rotation. Instead of the same people picking and dropping off the money and product, we gonna rotate the people and rotate the days. That way the only people who know about the pick-up and drop off will be me, Nick and the nigga doing the run ight?" Trey said.

Everyone nodded their head. There was nothing else to talk about, so we all headed out.

"Trey, come ride with me to go pick up Ny's Christmas gift."

"I'ma follow you, so that you don't gotta drop a nigga off when you're on your way home."

"Ight" I said.

I got in the car and just put on the radio. I was vibin to the music just thinking. These last couple of months that I been with Ny had been just what a nigga needed. I knew that I wanted to spend the rest of my life with her. She mad a nigga want to do better for the both of us. That's why I was having a spa built that was gonna be just for Ny. Next year she would be graduating with her Bachelor's degree in business. So, why not put her degree to use in her own business? I pulled up to Harry Winston on 5th Avenue. I waited about five minutes for Trey to get there.

"My nigga, you drive slow as fuck." I told him when he got out of the car.

"What nigga, what are we doing here?" He asked.

"This is where I got to pick up Ny's present from." I told him as we walked in the door.

"That's crazy cause I have to get Diamond's present from here, too."

It was crazy how much we thought alike. We walked up to the counter and told the lady that we was there to pick up. She got our names and went into the back.

"What did you get Ny?"

"You'll see."

As soon as I said that, the lady came back with our packages. We both paid her and left. When we got outside, I showed Trey what I got for Ny.

"Man, that shit is beautiful. I know that cost you a pretty penny." Trey said.

"It did, but it's for Ny, so money ain't a thang."

I asked him what he got for Diamond, but he said I will find out on Christmas. I laughed at him cause he went hard for me to show him Ny's gift, but he didn't wanna show me Diamond's. We dapped each other up and left. When I got home, Ny was curled up in the bed with her butt sticking out. I swear just the sight of her could make my dick hard. Ny didn't know it yet, but I planned on getting her ass pregnant the next time we had sex. I didn't see a reason not to. We were already living together, so why not have a baby running around the house. Tonight I would let her sleep.

I striped out of my clothes and cuddled behind her. She backed her body into mine. I moved her hair out of the way and whispered I love you. She replied back in a mumble. This was it for me, this is what I loved to come home to.

I woke up the next morning to Ny in the kitchen cooking breakfast. Ny knew how to throw down in the kitchen, that's why I was ready to take the next step. Christmas wasn't coming fast enough for me this year. I guess cause I had a big surprise, and that day was going to change my life forever. I walked up to Ny and gave her a quick peck on the lips.

"That's all I get for cooking you breakfast?" She asked, pouting.

"Yea, I can't give you anything else until you done. I don't need you burning up my food."

"Boy, please, you know I don't burn shit. That is what you be doing."

"Oh, so, you trying play a nigga right."

"I'm just being honest."

"Yea ight, you know you love my cooking, stoop fronting," I told her.

"Yea, yea, yea, whatever, just hurry up and eat, so we can go to shopping."

"All you do is shop. Don't you have enough shit?" I asked her, grabbing my plate from her hands.

"Its winter break, and I have nothing to do. Oh and smart ass, I'm not going shopping for me, I'm getting the rest of the presents." She said, smacking the back of my head before I sat down.

"Yea, whatever, you just like to shop. You better stop putting your hands on me, I'll fuck you up, lil nigga." I mean mugged the shit out of her, so she knew I was serious.

"Boy, please, you won't hurt a fly. Now, hurry up and eat."

I just nodded my head at her and started eating my food. It was on sight for Ny. After we finished eating, I told Ny I would clean the kitchen while she got in the shower. I finished the dishes and crept up stairs. I opened the bathroom door, and Ny was rapping that Hot Boy song by Bobby Smurda. I left the bathroom to get a dish towel, when I got it, I twisted it up.

"If you ain't a hoe get up out my trap house!!!!!! Ouch WHAT THE FUCK" she yelled.

I kept hitting her with the twisted up towel.

"Nick, you better stop hitting me with that shit."

I paid her threats no mind

"Nick, I'm not playing! Fucking stop!"

I stopped hitting her with it and started dying laughing. The way she was trying to run from that towel reminded me of when we went to M&M world. She got out of the shower and went straight into the bed room. She moved around like a nigga wasn't even in the room, I don't know what she was mad for, she the one that said I wouldn't hurt a fly.

"Ny, what's your problem?"

She looked at me, gave me a stank face, and just kept doing what she was doing. I just shook my head. Ny was so fucking stubborn, she started the shit, and now she was mad cause I ended it, but I knew exactly what would have her acting right. She was about to pull her shirt over her head when I took it out of her hand and threw it on the floor.

"Nick, what are you doing now?" She asked.

I pushed her up against the wall and kissed her roughly. She tried to turn her head, but I put my hand underneath her chin and held her head straight. I reached my head down to see if she was wet, and her shit was leaking. I played with her just enough to where she was on the verge of cumming. and then, I stopped.

"Nick, get back over here and handle your business."

"No, you come handle your business." I told her as I lay on the bed.

She walked over to me and stripped me of clothes. She started kissing me, and then, her kisses got lower and lower. Ny never went down on me before, so I was ready to see what she was working with. She started just licking around the tip. Her mouth was moist as fuck. Then she started taking me inch by inch, until all 11 of my inches was in her mouth. Ny was sucking my shit like it was the last dick on earth, she kept rotating from sucking to slurping and from slurping to sucking. I could feel myself getting ready to release in her mouth, but I wasn't ready to do that just yet.

"Get on top, Ma." I told her.

She got on top and started working her hips. With every movement she made, she would grip my dick tighter. A nigga was gone off this shit. I grabbed on to her hips, so that I could dig deeper.

"Ahhhhh, this feels so good." She said in between moans.

"You ready to have my baby, Ny?"

"Mhmmm," she said.

"Nah, I want you to answer that shit." I told her, still grinding into her while she rode me.

"Yes" she said cumming.

"Yes what?" I asked.

"Yes, I'm ready to have your baby."

As soon as she said that, I flipped her over and gave her this dick. It wasn't long before she was cumming. Right after she did, I let loose. I got up so that I could get a rag and clean her up, and when I came back she was out. I guess going shopping was out of the question. I cleaned her up and then hopped in the shower. I didn't have shit to do today, so I just chilled until Ny woke up, so we could be out.

Nylah

If it's one thing Nick knew how to do, he knew how to lay that pipe. He knocked my little ass out. When I woke up, I found him in the living room watching Bad Boys 2. I got on the couch and snuggled up next to him.

"Sleeping beauty finally woke up I see." He said, kissing my forehead.

"Shut up, I wasn't sleep for that long."

"You wasn't, but you was knocked out though. I went in the room to check on you, and you was snoring all loud and shit."

"I do not snore." I told him.

"Ma, yes you do, that shit sounded crazy."

"Yea, right," I told him, laughing.

"I love you," he said, leaning in and kissing me.

"I love you, too." I told him.

We snuggled up and finished the rest of the movie before we got dressed and went to Soho.

Nick wanted to get a couple of things from the Adidas store, so I went with him. Nick was trying on some sneakers when the Mr. Chocolate from the mall walked up to me.

"Beautiful, we meet again." He said, showing off that pretty smile.

I knew I couldn't flirt like I did last time cause Nick would beat my ass and dude's ass.

"Yes, we do, but just like the last time, I am still spoken for." I told him

By now Nick was headed our way. I just knew some shit was about to pop off.

"Ny, who's your friend?" Nick asked, not even looking at me but looking at Mr. Chocolate.

"He's not my friend, he just came over here." I said, trying to defuse the situation.

"Yea, ight, let's go." Nick said, walking towards the door.

I was right behind him cause I didn't want no shit popping off.

"I hope you still have my number, beautiful." Mr chocolate said before we could get out the door.

Nick turned around so fast I thought I was seeing double.

"My mans, you can best believe if she had your number, she ain't got that shit no more." He said, getting in Mr. Chocolates face.

"No need to get all hostile, she told me she had a dude from the jump. I just gave her my number just in case shit didn't work out, you feel me."

"My nigga, this ain't what you want." Nick said, lifting up his shirt just a little.

"Nick, come on, let's go. This nigga ain't even worth it." I told him, trying to get him to walk away.

"You better listen to your girl." Mr chocolate said with a smirk on his face.

I could tell this shit wasn't gonna end well. Nick turned like he was leaving the store, then did a 180 and hit him with a two piece. I'm not gonna lie, I thought Mr.

Chocolate would have been knocked out. But these two niggas were going toe to toe in the fucking Adidas store. The manager came out talking about he was gonna call the cops if they didn't stop fighting now. I knew I wouldn't be able to get Nick to stop, so I went in my pursue and got out my .22 and fired a warning shot in the air. Everyone ran and ducked for cover. Both Nick and Mr. Chocolate went to go reach for their guns until they realized I was the shooter. I walked up to Mr. Chocolate with my gun aimed.

"If you ever, and I do mean ever, talk to me again, you won't have to worry about my nigga putting one in you cause I will do it on the spot." I said, and then walked out the door.

I was so fucking pissed and embarrassed. Nick came and got in the car about five minutes after me. I didn't know what he was still doing inside, but I really didn't give a fuck.

"Ny, that's what we doing now, taking people's fucking numbers?" He said, yelling.

"Nick, do not raise your voice at me. You heard him say I told him I was taken. What the fuck are you mad at?"

"I'm mad cause you out getting nigga's numbers and shit, and then that dark mutherfucker wants to try and press me about it." he said.

"Well, what do you want me to do?" I asked him.

He was starting to get on my nerves. I told dude I had a man, and maybe I shouldn't have took his number, but it was a little too late for that shit.

"Ny, I don't want you to do shit and give that damn gun. Why the fuck you always pulling that shit out?"

He had the nerve to question me about my gun, but he was just in there showing off his shit.

"Oh, so, you can show off your shit, but when I send a warning shot you wanna take my gun and shit."

"Ny, you sound fucking stupid. Yea, I showed that nigga my gun, but only he could see them shits. Your ass is on camera fucking shooting up the place." He yelled.

"Nick, stop fucking yelling at me. I'm not your fucking child."

"Your right, you not my fucking child. But I will tell you this, if I catch you with him, no fuck that, if I see the two of y'all on the same fucking block, I will not hesitate to kill you and his bitch ass."

I didn't say nothing else after that. I was so stuck on the fact that this nigga just threatened me that I didn't know what else to say. For the rest of the ride, I was quiet. When we got home, I went straight up stairs and slammed the door. I couldn't believe this shit, but at the same time, it was my own fault for taking his fucking number. I wasn't gonna cry over the situation cause it was what it was. If that was all it took for our relationship to be over, then so be it cause I didn't give a fuck. Nick's words replayed in my head again, I still couldn't believe he said he would kill me. Did he not know who I was? I didn't even know what 'who I was' meant, but I knew my middle name rang bells in the street.

Nick

I couldn't even be around Ny right now, I don't know what has got in to her, but recently she has been coming at me sideways. She must have thought I was soft or something cause of the way that I treat her. I was raised to treat women with respect, but the way she was acting, I wanted to put my hands on her. I called up Trey and told him that I was coming through, he said it was cool cause Diamond was staying with her mom tonight. I got to Trey's house in record time. I walked up to the door, and before I could knock, he opened the door.

"Nigga, why you pulling up screeching your tires and shit."

"Fuck all of that, you know what she had the nerve to do?" I said, walking into his house and going in the kitchen to pour me a drink.

"Who you talking about, Ny?" He asked.

I just gave that nigga the dumbest look I could.

"Who the fuck else would I be talking about."

"Man, I don't know. What happened though?"

"She wanted to go to Soho to go shopping for the rest of the Christmas presents. So while we down there, I was like 'let's go to the Adidas store'. We in the store, right, and I'm looking at some Jeremy Scotts. I pay for my shit, and when I go to tell Ny let's go, she got some fuck boy in her face and shit." I told him, taking my bottle of Henny and going in the living room.

"Damn, she didn't get disrespectful like that." He said, shaking his head.

"That's not even the half of it. I go over there, and this nigga tells me that she already told him that she got a dude, but he gave her his number just in case shit don't work out. Trey....you already know what I did next."

"What you do, nigga?"

"I hit that nigga with a two piece. We was going blow for blow when Ny pulled out her gun and told that nigga don't talk to her again."

"Damn, baby sis doing it like that. She too damn trigger happy." He said, laughing.

"Nigga, that shit ain't funny. I told her if I catch them two on the same fucking block I'ma kill them both. Ny don't know who she fucking with. Yea, I' m nice to her and shit, but I think she be forgetting who she be fucking with."

"Man, Ny ain't stupid, or at least I hope she ain't. But look, that's my sister, and you're my nigga, I don't want to have to get in the middle of this shit." He said.

I understood where he was coming from, but I meant what I said, if I saw them together they both was fucking dead. I just didn't give a fuck, if it was one thing that I hated, it was to be disrespected. That just wasn't something I could tolerate. I kicked it with Trey for the rest of the night. I had no intentions of going home any time soon.

Chapter 8

Diamond

It was finally Christmas day. I was busy trying to finish cooking everything before everyone got here. Ny said she would come over early and help me, but her ass has yet to show up. Trey was in the living room getting all the presents ready. I was so excited; I just hoped that everything turned out good. Ny and Nick seemed to be getting along after the shit that happened in Soho. I just wish that they could get their shit together.

"Trey," I yelled.

"Yea, ma wassup," He said, walking into the kitchen.

"I need you to watch this. I have to go upstairs and get dressed. Everyone should be coming soon."

"Ma, you look fine, you can stay just like that."

This boy must have been crazy. I had on a pair of sweat pants and a damn 2pac t-shirt.

"Boy, you bugging."

"Sweat pants, hair tied, chilling with no make-up on, that's when you're the prettiest, I hope that you don't take it wrong," he rapped in my ear.

"Trey, you are some type of crazy, now will you just watch this while I go get ready."

He nodded his head yes and spanked me on my ass. I was about to walk upstairs when Trey called my name.

"Diamond."

"Yes, Trey," I said.

"I love you," he said.

At first, I was kind of stuck because I didn't know he felt that way. I didn't even know that's where we was at in our relationship.

"It's okay if you don't say it back, Diamond. I just wanted you to know how I felt." He said smiling at me.

I smiled back and took my ass upstairs. Why didn't I say it back? I already knew that I loved him, and I told him once already. But why when he said it did I freeze up? I didn't want to dwell on it too much because today was supposed to be a happy day for family and friends. When I came back downstairs everyone was already here but Jay. I didn't really want her to come, but she was Trey's mom, so how could I not invite her? She just rubbed me the wrong way. It was like she was trying way too hard to be their mom, when it should have just come naturally, but that was none of my business. I said hi to everyone before I went in the kitchen to check on the food.

"Don't leave me in there with all them, man." Ny said, coming in the kitchen with me.

"Ny, my mother is in there, you could have stayed and talked to her." I told her.

"Nah, I'm cool, you need any help?"

"You was supposed to be over here earlier to help me. Now everything is damn near done, and you want to help."

"I'm sorry, boo, I was coming until Nick wanted to start some shit."

"I thought y'all was good."

"We ight. I can tell he still a little salty about what happened, but he will be just fine. And when I say he wanted to start some shit, I meant as in trying to have a little him running around." She said.

"He trying to knock you up, huh," I said.

I already knew what the deal was. When a nigga knocked a female up, he felt as though she belonged to him, and that they would always have some type of ties to each other, just in case the female up and left his ass.

"He trying, I know what he doing though. He trying to get me pregnant, so I can be on locked down. But little do he know, a baby isn't gonna stop this show. Plus, I been thinking about opening my own business, maybe like a spa or a salon. We graduate soon, and I want to put this damn degree to use. What do you think?"

"Ny, I think it's a good idea, if you ever need a partner, let me know."

We continued talking while setting the table up. Everyone wanted to open presents, so that's what we did before we ate.

Me and Trey gave out our presents first. We got a Nick an all-black Presidential Rolex. Next up was my mother; we got a gift certificate to Spa Castle and about 4 new Michael Kors bags. Jay wasn't there yet, so we just put her gift to the side. We gave Pops money cause there was really nothing we could get him cause he already had it all. Last was Ny, we got her 2 Michael Kors bags, a charm bracelet from Tiffany's, and Trey gave her 50gs. Before me and Trey could exchange gifts, he wanted to make a speech first.

"I thank all you guys for coming and celebrating Christmas with us. As you know, Diamond is pregnant with my baby, and that is already the best Christmas present I could ask for. So, being the nigga that I am, you know I had to out-do her." He said, handing me a box.

When I opened the box, I was amazed at what I saw. Inside was a 6 carat, diamond, tennis bracelet. But what made it so special was the fact that it had a T and a D pendant hanging off of it. In the middle of our two initials, was the name Arielle, which is what we was going to name our daughter.

"Oh my God! This is beautiful, baby." I said with tears in my eyes.

"Your man did good, huh?" He asked, helping me put it on.

"Oh, shut up." I handed him the keys to a red and black Ducati 848 Street fighter.

"Ma, you didn't," he said jumping up.

"It's parked at Ny's house, so you got to wait to pick it up." I told him

"Come on, you can't be serious. Nick you couldn't have brought it over here for me, my nigga?"

"Nah Diamond told me not to and she crazy like Ny's ass so I wasn't getting on her bad side." Nick said.

While everyone else was giving out their gifts, Trey was sitting there with a pout on his face. This nigga was a big ass baby, but I loved him none the less. We was all ready to eat when Jay called and said that she was five minutes away. It was about time she got her ass here cause we damn sure was going to eat without her.

Jay

I was running a little late for all the festivities because I had a meeting that just couldn't be rescheduled. I called and told them I was on my way, when I was about to get out of the car, my cell phone rang.

"Hello," I said into the phone, kind of annoyed because all I wanted to do was spend time with my family.

"Everything is straight, right?" The guy on the other side of the phone asked.

"Yea, everything is a go for tonight." I told him back

"Ight, cool, I'll let you know when it's handled."

"Just don't fuck this up." I told him and hung up.

I walked in the house, and everyone was in the living room laughing and joking around. This was really a sight to see.

"Hey, everyone," I said.

"Wassup Jaz, it's about time you got here." Pops said.

"Yea, Jay, it took you long enough." Trey said, laughing.

"Y'all better leave my mother alone before it be a problem," Ny said.

"That's right, baby, let them know." I told her.

They all got up and gave me a hug. After the

greetings were over, I gave everyone their gifts. I got each of them something special and something that I thought they would like. Everyone seemed happy with their gifts, so we went to the table to eat. We all sat down and started passing the dishes around so that we could fill our plates.

"So, Jay, did you think about moving back to Brooklyn?" Diamond asked.

"Yea, I thought about it. I'm still not sure, cause the Maxwell family hasn't made their move yet."

"Fuck them pussy niggas, they don't want beef with us." Trey said, acting just like his father.

Knight was a real hot head back in the day. You couldn't tell that man nothing, when someone wanted to go to war with him, it was a war that he brought.

"Y'all shit is going good, y'all are the niggas to see. I don't want to fuck that up with my bullshit."

"But ma, if you move back, it would mean a lot to me, I feel like I would actually have my mother back."Ny said.

"I don't know, let me think about it." I said, ending the conversation.

Moving back is something that I wanted, but at the same time, I was trying to look out for my family, and me being far away was the best thing for them.

Ratatatata!!!!!!!!!!!!

"Niggas don't know how to act on holidays though," Ny said.

We all laughed and shook our heads on agreement. I was the first one to see the bullet go through the window.

"DUCK!!!!!!!" I yelled.

The shots were coming from every direction. We told Diamond and Nylah to get upstairs. I pulled out my gun and made it to the door with Trey, Pops and Nick behind me. By the time we got outside, the black Impala was speeding down the street. We ran to the front of the yard and started shooting. Nick blew out the two back tires, and the car crashed. We ran up on the car with our guns drawn. If they thought they was gonna shoot up my family's house and everything would be alright, they had another thing coming. There were three guys in the car. We pulled them out and brought them back to the house. Trey's house had a basement, so we tied them up and left them down there. We went back upstairs to check on the girls. I told Trey and Nick to go upstairs while me and Pops made some phone calls. Niggas were gonna pay for this, if it was the last thing I do.

Nylah

I didn't know what the hell was going on. One minute we at the table eating, then we hear gun shots, and then, them same bullets are coming through the kitchen window. My heart has never beat so fast in my life. I thought I was about to die, I kind of felt like it was karma coming to bite me in the ass for what I did to Jacob. I still haven't gotten over that. I know that I act all tough, but I still had nightmares about that night. I didn't tell Nick cause I didn't want him to worry about me.

"Are y'all alright?" Trey asked, coming into the room with Nick right behind him.

"Yea we cool, what the fuck was that?" Diamond said.

"I'm not sure, but we bout to find out. We got three niggas downstairs. Y'all are gonna go to Nylah's house while we handle shit." Nick said.

"What are y'all gonna do about that crashed car out there, you know by now someone already called the police." I said.

"Don't worry bout it, we got that covered." Nick said.

Nick wanted to walk me to my car while Diamond packed a small bag. When we got downstairs, I hugged my mother so tight that I didn't wanna let go. I didn't wanna experience losing my mother all over again after I just got her back. I told my mom I loved her and gave pops a hug before I went to go get in my car. While waiting for Diamond, Nick passed me a small black box.

"Nick, what's this?" I asked him.

"I was gonna wait until we got home to give you your last Christmas gift. But seeing how things turned out, we are gonna have a full house tonight. Just open the box." He said.

I opened the box, inside was a 9.5 carat cushion cut diamond ring. I almost died, it was so beautiful. I felt tears welling up in my eyes.

"Nylah, I loved you since I first saw you. I'm not gonna make a whole speech cause what's understood doesn't have to be explained." He said.

"You're so silly," I said, laughing.

I had to laugh at that last part cause he was a damn fool.

"Nylah Royce Taylor, will you marry me?" He asked, looking deep into my eyes.

I felt like he was looking deep into my soul. It was like he was looking for himself in me, and the fact that he asked me to marry him tells me that he found himself.

"Yes!!!!!!!!!!!!!!!" I yelled.

We shared a passionate kiss. But it wasn't like any other kiss that we had shared before. This kiss felt different.

"Ugh, no one wants to see that." Trey said.

"Stop hating." I told him.

"Me and my boo can do that, too, right Diamond?" Trey said, trying to give Diamond a kiss.

"Trey, back up," Diamond said, pushing him away.

"I see how it is."

"You know I'm playing, now, come give me a kiss."

"That's how you got pregnant in the first place, now, Diamond, let's go." I said.

Diamond hopped in the car, I kissed Nick goodbye and waved at Trey. I wasn't so sure I wanted to share my good news because of what happened, and what was gonna happen once we left the house. Me and Diamond both knew that those three guys weren't walking out of that house alive. The ride to my house was quiet. I guess we was both in our own thoughts. I knew this had to be stressful for Diamond cause she was pregnant and just really opened up to Trey. It was safe to say that we just couldn't get a break. No matter how happy we was, there was always somebody trying to fuck it up.

Nick

It was fucking Christmas, and we had to deal with this shit. Once we made sure that Ny and Diamond got to the house safely, we went downstairs to handle business. By now, the three guys were conscience. We all just stood in front of them.

"What the fuck y'all looking at?" one of them asked.

We all just laughed. This guy had some nerve. Here he was tied up, and he was asking questions.

"You come to my house and shoot up shit while my family is there, and you asking me what the fuck are we looking at?" Trey yelled.

"Calm down," Jay said.

"We already know that we ain't getting out of here, and y'all ain't getting no info out of us, so you might as well just kill us." The same guy said.

POW!

Jay shot him right in between his eyes, brains splattered on the other two dudes.

"Now, before you two end up looking like y'all friend, I'm gonna ask you one question, and one question only. Who, the fuck, sent y'all to shoot at my family?" I said.

Neither one of them said anything, so I cocked my gun back, getting their attention.

"Maybe y'all didn't hear me. Who told y'all to come here?"

"Ight, Ight. It was Javon." One of the guys said.

"Who the fuck is Javon?" Trey asked.

"Javon is the head of the Maxwell family." Pops said.

"How did he know where we was going to be?" Trey asked

They both looked at Jay and then back at us. One of them was about to say something when Jay shot the both of them.

"Why the fuck did you just do that? They was about to tell us how they knew where the fuck we was." I yelled at her.

She didn't reply, she just walked out of the room.

"What the fuck was that about?" Trey said.

Pop just shook his head, and we went upstairs to find Jay. She has some explaining to do, the nigga was just about to drop the dime, and she killed them. When we got upstairs, she was throwing back a shot.

"Jay, what was that back there?" Trey asked.

"What was what?"

"You shot them before we could find out how they knew where we was going to be at." I said.

"It didn't matter how the fuck they knew where we was going to be at. The more important thing was who sent them." she said.

Me and Trey just stared at her, I knew that she was Ny's mom, but she was wildin' for real.

"She's right, Javon is well connected. He can get any information that he wants; just like Jay is very connected." Pops said.

"Yea whatever, they came at the wrong niggas today though and that's facts." I said, getting even more heated.

"Calm down, young blood, we gonna get at these niggas, and I'm moving to back home. I thought I was protecting my family by staying away, but they brought the war to y'all, so now, we are gonna end it." Jay said, getting up and leaving.

"Y'all are about to see a side of Jay y'all never seen before, just be ready." He said before leaving too.

Me and Trey both downed a shot before we called the clean-up crew. We rode in silence. We both knew what was gonna happen next. There was no need to speak on it. Brooklyn was about to be painted red.

Chapter 9

Elle

Tonight was the night that I was going to put my plan in motion. I haven't talked to Ny since that day we got into it in her car. She didn't even try to reach out or nothing. That's how I knew that what I had planned was the right thing to do. I was tired of being Nylah's door mat. Whenever she needed something, I was there. I was there to pick up the pieces to her heart when Jacob broke it. I was there when she found out that her mom was alive again, but she still just walked all over me like I was nothing.

Ny meant the world to me, I would do anything for her, but that wasn't enough. But today was the day that I got back at her and Nick. I heard about Nick and Trey killing everything moving that they thought was associated with the Maxwell family. I thought that because Brooklyn was on lock, Ny was going to cancel Nick's birthday bash. Shit, was I wrong, she still was going through with it. I hated that about her, when it came to Nick, she would do anything necessary to make him happy while she gave the rest of us her ass to kiss.

"Hey, baby," Bee said, kissing me on my cheek.

Me and Bee have been hanging tight lately, I truly felt bad for the way I treated her.

"How did you sleep?" I asked her.

"Great."

"You ready for tonight."

"Yea, but are you sure this is going to work?" she asked me.

"Don't worry, all you have to do is get this video to the DJ, and I will do the reset." I told her, kissing her.

"Stop, Elle, not right now," she said, trying to move away from me.

"Come on, Bee, let me taste that honey." I told her
nibbling on her ear.

"Elle, no, I have to go home and get ready."

"Okay, okay, but tonight your mine." I told her,
slapping her on her butt as she went into the bedroom.

While she got dressed, I decided to watch the video
that everyone in Brooklyn was going to see tonight.

"Why are you watching that video again?" Bee asked
me

"No reason, I just wanted to make sure that
everything was perfect." I told her.

"Yea, right, just give me the video, so I can get
going."

I gave her the video and walked her to the door. I
kissed her good bye and watched her drive off. I think today
was one of the happiest days of my life. By the end of
tonight, Ny's relationship will be over, cause like I said, if I
couldn't have Ny, then no one could.

Nylah

I have been running around all day trying to get
everything ready for Nick's party. Since Christmas he and
Trey have been running wild, killing everything moving. So
far, there has been 12 deaths in the last week. Now, I'm not
sure that Nick did it, but I don't think that he didn't. It took
me forever to get him agree to having this party. It was bad
enough him and Trey would barely let us out the house by
ourselves. I could understand where they was coming from,
but damn, we did have lives. On top of that, our holiday
vacation was coming to an end soon, so we would have to go
back to school. I haven't heard from Elle in a while, but I
wasn't going to call her either, after what she said to me I was
good on her ass. I did miss her though, but how could I
forgive her after she slept with Jacob. That was a line that

should have never been crossed. I had to go pick up Diamond, so we could go and get our hair and nails done.

"Diamond, you shouldn't be going to no party, your ass is seven months pregnant." I told her when she and my mom got in the car.

"Bitch, please, I want to go and shake something. I'm lying, I just want to chill and vibe that's it."

"I'm surprised Trey didn't kick your ass for trying to go."

"He didn't want me to go at first, but then I told him I would be home alone." Diamond said.

I started dying laughing I couldn't believe that she had played that card.

"Diamond, you ain't got no shame." I told her.

"What you mean? I didn't do nothing." she said, smiling.

When we got to the hair shop, it was busy as usual. We chilled and listened to the gossip that was going around. The people in this shop talked about everything and everyone, this is way I didn't spread my business because as soon as you told one person everyone knew. Me and Nick still haven't told anyone that we were engaged, I didn't even wear my ring. We was waiting until all this bullshit was over with, so that we could really enjoy it. It was finally our time to get our wigs done. I wanted something different, so I told my girl Kelly to die my hair burgundy. Diamond just went with a simple Dominican blow out, but me, I wanted something drastic. When Kelly was done with my hair, I almost fainted, I loved it.

"Kelly, you slayed that," Diamond said.

"Yea, you did your thing. Ny that color looks beautiful on you." My mom said.

"Thanks y'all, and Kelly, you did your thing as usual. Here you go, mama."

I handed her the money with a nice tip. Whenever I needed my hair done, I went to Kelly. She was the only chick

I trusted to do my hair. After we got our hair done, we went and got our nails done. While our nails was drying, my phone chirped, letting me I had a text message. When I looked at my phone, it was a text from Nick.

Bae: Where you at ma

I texted him back, telling him that we was at the nail salon, and I that I would be home soon. He told me that he had Trey with him so bring Diamond with me.

"Trey and Nick are at the house. They want us to go home when we done." I told Diamond.

"Okay, but one of them are cooking cause I'm starving."

"You're always hungry. What else is new? Let's go" I told her.

On the way home, we talked about the baby and decided that we needed to start planning the baby shower. Diamond and Trey had asked me and Nick to be the God parents, so we had to go all out for our baby. When we got to the house, we smelled food. We walked into the kitchen and found Trey and Nick cooking.

"Oh, shit, is that Nick and Trey in the kitchen cooking?" Diamond asked, sitting at the table.

"I don't know, maybe we walked into the wrong house." I said, laughing.

"Why y'all always trying to clown us? Ny you already know I can cook cause I cooked you breakfast the first time I put my name on it." he said, winking at me.

"Eww y'all are so nasty," Diamond said.

They made our plates and sat down with us. I'm not gonna lie, this food looked good. They made us baked chicken, rice, and corn on the cob. We was some lucky girls, cause not a lot of men could cook.

"Mhmmm this is good," Diamond said.

"Yea, it is." I said agreeing.

"We just wanted to do something nice for y'all. We know we really haven't been around lately cause we been ripping and running the streets. But we been doing it for y'all. We just want to keep you three safe." Trey said.

"Well, thank you, it is really appreciated. Just don't go to the party in all black like y'all ready for war, okay." I said, causing everyone to laugh.

For the rest of the afternoon, we just chilled with each other and watched TV.

Nick

Today was my 25th birthday, I thanked God that I was able to see this age cause for a while I thought I wasn't going to make it past 21. I didn't want Nylah to throw this party at first because of this whole Javon thing. We have been fucking shit up, looking for him, and no one has even heard of this nigga. We figured we could take a break for my birthday. Since everyone was already at the house, we decided to go together. Me and Ny went upstairs to get ready while Trey and Diamond stayed downstairs.

"Come on, Trey, your worse then a girl!" Ny yelled.

"Ny, I know you're not complaining. You take damn near an hour just to do your damn hair."

"Whatever, don't hate, I have to make sure I'm flawless when I step out."

"Ma, you know your flawless, regardless if you did your hair or not." I told her, kissing her.

"Awww, you're so sweet; now move," she said, trying to push me out of the bathroom.

Since it was my birthday, you know me and my crew had to show out. We was all dressed in black and gold.

"Damn, y'all ready yet." Trey yelled up stairs.

"I'm waiting for Ny's slow ass." I said walking downstairs.

"Shit, for all that time she took, she better look like Halley Berry." He said.

"OR BEYONCE!!!!!" we all yelled.

"Y'all got jokes." Ny said, coming down the stairs.

"Girl, you know you take forever," Diamond said.

"You take as long as me," Ny said, pouting.

"Awww, leave my baby alone." I said, coming to Ny's rescue.

"That's why her ass is spoiled now." Trey said.

We all piled into my big boy Escalade. I didn't drive it much, only on special occasions. We pulled up to Webster Hall, and the line was around the corner. We got out, and all eyes were on us.

"Wassup, Jones," I said to the bouncer.

"Nick, my man," he said, dapping me.

I slipped him 200 to let me and Trey bring out guns in. With all this shit going on, I didn't wanna get caught slipping. We walked in and went right to the third floor where the V.I.P. Section was. Ny did the damn thing. The whole club had black and gold balloons that had my name on it. When we got to our section, there were already bottles on the table. Jay and Pops were already there, and from the looks of it they already got the party started.

"Happyyyyyy Birthdayyyyy Nick," Jay slurred, giving me a hug and a kiss.

"Thanks. You ight though?"

"Yea, I'm turnt up, boy, you better act like you know," she said, doing a little dance.

I have never seen Jay like this. But I guess everyone needed a break from all the hectic shit that was going on.

"Happy birthday, son," Pops said, giving me a hug.

"Thanks," I told him.

I grabbed a bottle and started enjoying my night. The club was jumping. Ny said she wanted to dance, so she took me to the lower level. When we got down there, she turned around towards me and whispered happy birthday. As soon as she said that, I heard Jay-Z's "Tom Ford" start playing.

Clap for a nigga with his rapping ass. Blow a stack for your niggas with your trapping ass. Clap for a nigga with his rapping ass. Blow a stack for your niggas with your trapping ass. Tom Ford.

Me and Ny was going in, rapping along, but then the music stopped, and it sounded like he was rapping live. I looked up to see my nigga on stage going in. Ny outdid herself with this one. After he did his set, me and Ny went back to our V.I.P. Section and just chilled. Ny said she had one more surprise for me, and that she would be right back. I didn't know what else she was going to do. The only thing I wanted was her naked and in my bed.

Nylah

So far, Nick was enjoying his birthday. I know he acted like it was nothing when Jay-Z hit the stage, but I know that nigga hype. He was just trying to keep it cool and gangsta. I had one last surprise for him. It was a video of all his pictures, showing off his journey so far. I gave the DJ my flash drive, and when I was walking back to where Nick was, I bumped into Elle.

"So, you can't speak to your best friend anymore?" She said.

"After you slept with Jacob, you would never be my best friend." I told her and began walking away.

"Well, just tell Nick I said happy birthday, and that I hope he likes the video."

I didn't know what she was talking about, and I didn't care either. Tonight was all about Nick, and nothing or no one could fuck that up.

"If I could get everyone's attention, tonight is my big homie Nick's birthday, and his wife threw him this party that y'all are enjoying so much. Shit, she even paid for the open bar, so y'all better enjoy that. The only thing she asks is that you share this moment with them as y'all watch Nick's rise as the king of the thrown." The DJ said.

He started the video, and at the beginning there was a picture of Nick as a baby, and then, it went on to his teen years. After that, a video came on. I was confused cause I never put no video in the slide show. The video started off with me walking towards the camera in a trench coat. Then I dropped the coat, and there I was all in my naked glory. Everyone gasped at the scene. After that, it switched to a scene of me riding the dick backwards, and when it showed the face of my partner, I damn near died. The person in the video with me was Jacob.

I turned to look at Nick, and his face was red. He had a look on his face that I have never seen before. He stormed over to the DJ booth, ripped out all the plugs and told everyone to get the fuck out. I wanted to follow him, but I was too scared. That video was from a year ago when I was dating Jacob. He somehow convinced me to record one of our sexcapades. What blew my mind was that the date that was on the bottom left corner of the video was three months ago. I didn't know how this could be possible when I haven't fucked Jacob since we broke up. I got up to try and explain this to Nick when I spotted Elle making an exit. At that moment, I knew that her sneaky ass had something to do with it. Especially from that comment she made earlier.

"Elle, why the fuck would you do that?" I asked her, walking all in her personal space.

"I don't know what you're talking about." She said with a smirk.

At that point, I lost it. I threw my fist back and punched her dead in her face. She stumbled a little, but she came right back, throwing two rights. I dodged them both and kept swinging. She slipped on liquor that was spilled on the floor, and I was on her ass like white on rice. I was beating the shit out of her when I felt someone picking me up. I threw my head back, head butting them and went right back to fucking Elle up. I didn't care about anything at that moment except for the fact that my best friend betrayed me.

I was beating Elle unconscious when someone else picked me up off her. I was too tired to head butt this guy, so I just let him carry me out. The person threw me in the car and got in the front seat. I turned to see that it was Nick. He started the car and just drove off. The entire ride he didn't look my way or say anything. I felt a little uncomfortable because I didn't know where to begin to fix the situation. I knew how it looked, and I knew that if the roles were reversed, I would probably be doing the same shit he was doing but worse. He pulled up to the house and simply said get out. I was stuck, I didn't wanna get out because I felt like if I got out I would never see him again. But I knew not to play with him right now.

"When you're ready to let me explain, just let me know. Just know what you saw is not what it seems. I love you Nick, and I would never do anything that would ruin what we have."

He just shook his head. I felt like at least that was a start. I got out of the car and watched him pull away. Walking up to the house I shared with Nick felt like the longest walk of my life. I went right upstairs, got in my bed and cried. I lost the love of my life all because I had a deceitful friend. I swear that when and where ever I saw Elle, it was going to be on sight for her ass.

Nick

What started off as a good birthday, ended in a shitty one. I was seeing red, and I was ready to hurt something. Everyone kept calling my phone, trying to see what the move was. There was nothing to move on cause Jacob's ass was already dead. What I wanted to know was, who the fuck set

that shit up for me to see. Someone wanted me to see that
video, and they wanted to humiliate Ny, cause they showed it
at the party. My phone started vibrating, letting me know that
I had another phone call. I was gonna send it to voice mail
when I saw that it was Trey.

"Yo wassup," I said into the phone.

"You ight, man," he asked.

"I should be asking are you okay? Ny fucked you up,
son."

"Man, that ain't nothing. She wild though, she was
fucking Elle up."

"Yea, I know, I didn't even find out why. I was too
pissed off to even look at her."

"That shit was crazy, you know we gonna handle
whoever played that shit though, don't even stress."

"You already know. I'm bout to go hit up this bar
until I'm ready to go home, if I choose to even go home."

I had to shake my head cause Ny really fucked up.

"Go home and talk to Ny. You don't need to be
drinking alone anyway." Trey said.

"Nah, I wanna be alone. I'll hit you up tomorrow."

I hung up and got out of my car. I pulled up to some
hole in the wall bar on Flatbush Avenue. I walked in and
everything seemed cool, so I sat in the corner and told the
waitress to keep them coming. I know I shouldn't have been
drinking alone, but fuck it a nigga wanna be alone right now.
I was throwing them drinks back, shot after shot. I was trying
to forget the bullshit that happened tonight. I lost track of
time, and by the time I looked at my watch it was 4 in the
morning. I still wasn't ready to go home, but I was starting to
feel light headed, and my vision got blurry. A cute brown
skin chick came and sat next to me.

"Hey, are you okay," she asked

I shook my head yea cause my words was coming out
slurred. She started saying how she was going to take me
home cause I shouldn't be in the bar like this cause someone

could take advantage of me. I laughed at shawty, or at least I thought I did. Something was wrong. I kept going in and out of it. When we got outside the bar, she asked where my car was, and I just pointed. We walked over to the car, and she dug in my pockets for my car keys. I was glad that she came and helped me cause the way that I was fucked up I doubt I would have made it home. I typed my address into the GPS before everything went black.

Chapter 10

Brielle

Ny got my ass good, but I bet I got her ass one better. Even if Nick took her back after explaining to him what I did, I doubt she would take him back after finding out what he did. After someone got Ny off of me, I was rushed to the hospital. The doctor told me that I had a fractured rib, a broken arm, and my left eye was swollen shut. She said it would be sometime, but that I would make a full recovery. I knew once Ny told Nick what I did that them niggas was gonna come gunning for me, so I knew I had to get away and lay low for a while. I planned on going down south as soon as I was released from the hospital, and Bee came to pick me up. She had called me after the doctor gave me the news. She said that everything went perfectly. I was on cloud nine when she told me that, even though Ny had beat the shit out of me, but the shit that was about to come her way was well worth it. I don't give fuck what anyone has to say about my actions either. I played second fiddle long enough, now it was my turn to shine. I tried to love her, but it wasn't good enough, so call me a lover scorned. Shit, you could even call me the snake in the grass that bitches gotta look out for. Either way, I was gonna play karma, and everyone was gonna get what was coming to them.

Nick

I woke up the next day at five in the afternoon. My head was pounding. This shit didn't feel like a regular hang over. I can't even remember what happened after I got in the car. Shit, I wasn't even in my own damn bed. I was at some fucked up motel. I checked my pockets, and everything was still there, so the chick that drove me home didn't rob me. I went into the bathroom to splash some water on my face. I noticed there was a note on the sink.

Your phone kept going off while you was sleep in the car last night, so I looked at it. You had a lot of missed calls and texts from someone saved in your phone as wife. I figured you really didn't wanna go home, so I dropped you off at the motel. I know it's not nothing special, but it was all that I could afford. I wish we could have met under different circumstances, but here is my number just in case you ever need another designated driver. 718-863-1947

Bee
I was gonna her tell her thank you for getting a nigga somewhere safe. But I didn't like the fact that she went through my phone. I still wasn't ready to go home and talk to Ny. I figured I would check into a hotel until I was ready. I got in my car and turned on the radio. I didn't really wanna be left to my thoughts. Chris Brown's song "Loyal" came on, and I turned it all the way up. This is how I was feeling right now. Ny had something that chicks would die to get, and her ass wants to go and fuck her ex. It was cool though, cause like my nigga, CB, said, these hoes ain't loyal. I booked my room for a month, I didn't know if I was going to stay there for a month, but I knew it was possible. I hopped in the shower and just relaxed for the day. I hit Trey up, letting him know where I was at, and that I was good. I decided to call up that chick, Honey, and she what she was doing. I wasn't trying to fuck or nothing, I just wanted to someone to chill with.

"Hello," she said into the phone.
"Wassup, is this Honey?"
"Yea, this is she "
"This is Nick from last night, well, more like this morning. I was just calling you to tell you thank you."
"No need to thank me. I was just doing what seemed

to be the right thing."

"There's not a lot of people that would do that, ma, so again, thank you."

"Well, you welcome."

There was an awkward pause on the phone. I didn't know if I should invite her over or not. Shit, I didn't even know if I was single or not.

"Hello, you still there?" she said.

"Yea, I'm still here. I was just thinking how you would look sitting next to me in the Jacuzzi."

"You upgraded that motel already. And as good as that sounds, I'm actually going out of town."

"Oh ight ma."

"But we can still keep in touch, if you want."

"Yea, that will be cool. I'm a let you go though, have fun on your trip." I told her.

"Thanks, and don't be a stranger, Nick." she said and hung up.

I wasn't sure what that was all about, but even though I still loved Ny, I didn't feel guilty about Honey. Maybe this is what we needed from each other; a break. Maybe we just jumped into everything a little too fast.

I was tired of thinking about that bullshit, so I ordered room service and just watched TV. My phone kept vibrating, so I turned it off. I figured I would get back to the real world tomorrow, but for now, I was just gonna chill and relax.

Nylah

I have been calling Nick's phone ever since I woke up. I just needed to talk to him. I know I told him to come to me when he was ready to let me explain, but fuck that, I needed to explain now. I talked to Trey, and he said that Nick was fine. He was staying at some hotel. I was glad that he was safe, but I didn't want him at no hotel. I wanted him with me. Thinking about the whole situation had me ready to go over to Elle's house and kick her ass again. This shit was all her fault; all because she couldn't understand that I didn't want to be with her ass. I should have just left her ass alone the first time she tried some shit, but no, I had to be a good friend and give her another chance.

Someone at the door interrupted my rant. I went to go see who it was, but when I got there they were gone, but they left a manila envelope on my door step. At first, I wasn't going to touch it cause it could have been anything in there, and on top of that, we still haven't found Javon. I called my mom to see what she thought I should do.

"Ny, does it look like a normal package?" my mom asked after I explained to her what happened.

"Yea, it looks fine. You know what, this is stupid, I'ma just check it out. I'll call you after I find out what it is." I said and hung up.

I don't know what I called her for cause if it was a bomb it would have went off already. I went out front and picked it up. When I opened the envelope, a DVD was inside. My blood started to boil. I felt like this was Elle playing games, and trying to make me relive what happened last night. I popped the DVD in and sat back.

At first the shit looked like someone was watching two people fuck in the car. I was about to turn it off when I saw the license plate on the car. I fast forwarded the video to make sure that I wasn't bugging. There was a brown skin girl, riding the shit out of Nick's dick. He had his head laid back, looking like he was enjoying it. You couldn't really see his face, the camera only showed the side of his face. Here I was crying because my, supposed to be, best friend did some fucked up shit and messed up my relationship. When my fucking fiancé is getting his dick wet only hours after he dropped me off. I picked up the DVD player and threw it at the TV. I was at a loss for words. I wasn't gonna cry or do no crazy shit. I was gonna sit and wait for him to bring his black ass here. I needed to vent to someone, so I called Diamond. She was in her final stages of her pregnancy, and I didn't wanna stress her out, but I had no one else to call.

"Diamond," I said as soon as she picked up the phone.

"Ny, what's wrong?"

"Diamond, he fucked some bitch last night."

"Nooo, how you know that?"

"Cause they sent the fucking video to my house."

"Oh, Ny, I'm sorry, boo. Do you need me to come over there?"

"Nah, I'm good. This whole thing is a mess. He didn't even let me explain about the video."

"What is there really to explain?" She asked.

"That the video was old, and some how Elle got a copy of it and changed the date stamp." I told her.

I know that sounded hard to believe, but it was the truth.

"Do you really think he is going to believe that? I'm not saying that it's not the truth cause I wouldn't put anything past Elle's ass. But that shit sounds crazy as hell." she said.

"I know it does, but that's the truth. Why you think I beat her ass last night?"

"You fucked her ass up, and you head butted Trey, too. You was acting a damn fool."

"I didn't even know that that was Trey. Damn, tell him I said sorry."

I felt bad about head butting him, but I was trying to fuck Elle up.

"He straight. Don't worry about it. But what are you gonna do about Nick?"

"I wanna beat his ass, but I'ma wait until he comes to me. I wanna see if all that I'm different stuff was true. I'ma act like nothing is wrong."

"Bitch, you crazy, I would have slashed somebody's tires, and then, found the bitch and slashed her face, too."

"Nah, see this way he digs a deeper hole for his self. Cause I can explain what he saw, but what he did to me, there is no explanation. When we first started dating, he was screaming how he is different, and how he would never hurt me and all this other bullshit. Now, I wanna see what he is gonna do." I told her.

We chatted a little while longer before I hung up the phone. I was over the whole crying shit. I was gonna keep doing what I had to do. School would be starting soon, and I had to focus on that. I couldn't let a heart break stop me from doing what I had to do. In the words of Lil Kim, FUCK NIGGAS GET MONEY.

Trey

I was worried about Nick and Nylah. Diamond said that she was throwing herself into her school and really hasn't been talking much. Nick just been going hard in the streets; between looking for Javon and handling business. Neither one of them wanted to talk to the other. They was getting on my fucking nerves. On top of that, I had to deal with Diamond and this pregnancy. I'm not saying that I'm not happy to be having a baby, but this shit was harder than I thought. The further along she got, the more she complained, and her mood swings were crazy. But like the true MVP I was, I was dealing with it all. I told Nick that I had to go pick up Diamond and take her to the doctor's office. He said he would ride with me. We walked in the house, and we herd laughter. As soon as we got to the kitchen it stopped. Ny and Nick just looked at the each other.

"So, I have to get going to my appointment," Diamond said, walking towards the front door.

I followed behind her cause I wasn't trying to get in the middle of that one.

"Do you think we should have left them there alone

like that?" Diamond asked me as we got in the car.

"Yea, they will be ight. They just need to talk. Ny gotta fix this shit."

"What you mean Ny gotta fix this? She didn't do anything wrong. Elle changed the date stamp on that video. The video was from a long time ago. Nick is the one fucking bitches in his car and shit."

"What you mean Nick was fucking some bitch?" I said.

I didn't think that Nick would do something that fucked up, he just wasn't the type.

"You heard what I said. He fucked some bitch in his car, and then, the bitch had the nerve to leave a DVD on Ny's doorstep. How could you let him do that shit?" she said, catching an attitude.

"What you mean how could I let him do that? He is his own man, I can't tell him what to do. Damn, I knew he was pissed off, but I didn't think that he would do that shit." I told her.

"Ny is gonna fuck him up. She said she just gonna play it cool and wait for him to tell her, but you know how Ny is. As soon as she gets pissed off, that shit is gonna come out." Diamond said.

"Well, that is really none of our business. Let them handle that shit." I told her.

As long as they didn't fuck up my house, I really didn't give a fuck what they did, or how they handled the situation.

Nylah

Damn he looked good, I thought, as he stood in front of me. We both have been sitting here since Trey and Diamond left not saying a word. I didn't wanna be the first to speak, but it looked like I was gonna have to.

"How you been?" I asked him.

"I'm cool, just doing what I have to do." He said.

"Okay." I said.

I wanted to get up and leave, but this is a conversation that we both needed to have. But he wasn't making this shit easy at all.

"Look, I just wanted to tell you that the video that you saw was from a while back when me and Jacob were dating."

"Ny, really though, that is the best you can come up with? There was a fucking date stamp on the video, and not to mention, I did walk in on him eating you out. So, how I know y'all wasn't fucking before that?"

"The only reason you saw Jacob eating me out was cause I was trying to look out for your fucking ass." I yelled.

"You wasn't looking out for nobody, you just wanted your pussy ate. It's cool, ma, you don't got to lie." He laughed, but it wasn't one of his normal laughs, it was more of a sinister laugh.

"Nick, fuck you, cause the same night that you saw that video, you fucked some bitch in your car."

"Ny, what the fuck are you talking about? That night I went to a bar and then went to a hotel."

"Nah, nigga, I seen the DVD. You had some bitch riding your dick in the car."

"You can't be serious, because your ass got caught out there on tape, you're gonna make up some shit. Come on, ma, you're better than that."

"You know what Nick, it doesn't even fucking matter. I fucking hate you, and just so you know, Elle fucked with the date stamp. That's why I was beating her ass that night." I told him.

I got up to leave, and the next thing I know, I was pinned against the wall.

"Ny, what did you just fucking say?" Nick asked me.

"I said I fucking hate you!" I yelled.

"Ny, you hate me, now, after you fucked up, you hate

me. You fucked that nigga, and let him tape it. So, how the fuck do you hate me?" He yelled.

I was starting to lose consciousness; he had his hand so tight around my neck. I was trying to loosen his fingers, but he wasn't letting go.

"Nick, stop, I can't breathe." I told him.

He removed his hands from around my neck, but then he forced me to look at him. I could feel the tears building up in my eyes. I couldn't stand to look him in his eyes. Every time I tried to look away, he would turn my head right back. All I saw in his eyes was hurt, and I was the cause of it. I couldn't stand the look that he had on his face, so I kissed him. I kissed him so passionately that it scared me. He turned me around and put my hands on the wall. He lifted my shirt and started putting kisses going down my back. He unzipped my jeans and bit my butt. I don't know if it was all the emotions, but I was turned on. He slid in from behind, and I gasped for air. He started going slow, with every thrust he went in deeper and deeper.

"Ahhh, Nick, yes, just like that."

He was hitting my spot every time he went deeper.

"Ny, who do you hate?"

I didn't wanna get into that right now, so I ignored him and just started throwing it back.

"Damn, Ny, chill, ma," Nick said, moaning.

He started to match my speed. The thrusts became faster and harder. I was in heaven.

"Yes, Nick, ohhhhh I'm coming," I yelled out.

After I came, I was spent. But I had to make sure Nick was taken care of. I started to tighten my muscles. Every time he would thrust out, I would suck him in deeper.

"Nylahhhh, fuck," he moaned as he started coming.

He leaned against me until he could catch his breath. Once he caught it, he pulled out, went upstairs, and about ten minutes later he came down and left. He didn't say nothing to me, he just walked out the door. I couldn't say that I blamed him, I know when I told him that I hate him I hurt his feelings. It seemed like I just kept screwing up the relationship, so maybe it wasn't him, maybe I was the problem in all of this.

Nick

Nylah had my mind all fucked up. When I went with Trey to pick up Diamond, I didn't expect to see Nylah there. I wasn't ready to talk to her just yet, but since she was there, why not get it out of the way. The shit that she said about Elle changing the date stamp kind of made sense, or at least Elle had something to do with it because Ny beat her ass. If it was true, I was gonna handle that situation, but then Ny started talking about me fucking another bitch. That I didn't know what the fuck she was talking about. She was stressing me out, every female said they want a good dude, and then, when they get one they wanna fuck shit up. Ny saying she hate me, hurt me. I swore I would never put my hands on her but when she said that, I lost it. I shouldn't have put my hands on her, and I shouldn't have had sex with her either. Shit was just fucked up, and I didn't know if I wanted to fix it. Yea, I loved Ny, she was my heart, but I couldn't deal with the bullshit anymore. I wasn't gonna do what most niggas do, and move on to the next chick when I was still caught up in another. But there was nothing wrong with me having a female friend. Me and Bee have been texting each other. It was nothing major, but she was cool and down to earth.

I been noticing that Jay has been acting funny. Ever since the drive by, we have been killing niggas left and right, looking for Javon, but it was like this nigga was a ghost. Jay said that she was all about keeping her family safe, but she hasn't been doing anything. A part of me was starting to believe that she was all talk. It seemed like there were too many snakes in the grass. I was gonna get to the bottom of everything because shit just wasn't adding up.

Diamond

I wanted to do something to try and cheer Ny up. She has been mopping around ever since we left her in the house with Nick. She didn't tell me exactly what happened, but I knew that it was something, because she acted like she didn't wanna leave the house. I had to come over and cook for her just so she could eat. I was eight months pregnant, and I couldn't really stand on my feet, so I wanted to take Ny out for lunch. She acted like she didn't wanna go, but once I said we was going to Red Lobster, she perked up. When we got there, we was seated right away. We ordered our food and just had idle conversation. I could tell that she didn't really wanna talk. The waitress came back with our food and we dug in.

"I am so glad you got me to come here cause this food is everything, and I was getting tired of your cooking." Ny said laughing.

"Whatever, you better be lucky that I came over there to cook for you stinking ass."

"You got jokes, but just know my ass never stinks."

"Yea whatever. I'm just happy that you're laughing and smiling again" I told her, and I honestly was.

"I know I been a lot to handle, and I'm sorry about it that. But I didn't forget about your baby shower, girl. We can start planning as soon as we get back." she said.

"No need to, it's already planned. We are having it Sunday. I just need you to cook." I told her.

"Okay, that's the least that I could do."

We was having a good time enjoying ourselves. We asked our waitress for the bill, but she said it had already been taken care of. Me and Ny just looked at each cause neither of us paid it.

"Who paid the bill?" Ny asked.

"It was that gentlemen over there," the waitress said and pointed to two tables behind us.

When me and Ny looked, it was Mr. Chocolate from the mall. I didn't know what it was, but this man just kept popping up.

We smiled at him and got up to leave. I didn't know what it was about Nylah, but this nigga had it bad for her. How you pay for a chick's lunch after she held a gun to your face? This nigga was on some fatal attraction type shit.

Demetri

It would be just my luck to run into her again. I saw her when she first walked in to the restaurant. I wasn't going to say anything to her because she pulled a gun out on me. But there was just something about her. I wanted her, and anything I wanted, I got. When the waitress left their table, I told her I would pay their bill and leave a big tip for her. Everything worked out, but instead of her coming over to say thank you, she just smiled and walked out the door. I couldn't let her get away that easily. I got up and followed her and her friend outside.

"Beautiful, are you ever going to tell me your name?" I asked her.

"The name is Nylah." She said.

"That's a beautiful name for a beautiful girl." I said.

"Thank you, but now I have to go." She said, walking away.

"Wait, I know this is crazy, but I can't get you off my mind. Let me take you out for dinner or something."

"You know what, here take my number cause for any nigga to wanna still talk to a chick after she put a gun in his face is really determined." She said.

"Oh shit, you must not be spoken for anymore."

"It's complicated right now. But I'm not looking for nothing more than a friend." She told me.

"That's fine, ma, everyone could use a friend, even

me."

"Ight, well, I'm bout to leave, so just text me....Oh yea what's your name?"

"Demetri," I told her.

She waved bye and took off. I didn't mind just being her friend, cause no one ever stays just friends. But if she wanted to play it like that, then I was down to play. I went back inside cause I was waiting to have a meeting with some nigga named Javon. He said he needed a problem handled, and that is what I did; handle problems. That's why I wasn't too worried about Nylah's man trying to get at me cause he ain't have shit on me. My murder game was something that niggas paid for, so knocking him off would be easier said than done.

"Yo, are you Demetri?" some nigga said, walking up to the table.

"Sit down, please." I told him.

He sat down, and I just stared at him. I had to figure out what type of nigga he was. He was well known in the streets, but sometimes what you heard in the streets isn't the truth. So, I had to analyze this nigga and make sure his credential was up to par.

"What could I do for you?"

"I have a problem. I'm trying to take over some territory, but these niggas are well connected. I have someone on the inside, but the person can only do so much."

"So, what is it exactly you are asking me to do?"

It sounded like this nigga was talking in circles.

"I need to you to kidnap someone for me."

"I don't do that kidnapping shit." I told him, standing up getting ready to leave.

"I know you don't, but I will make it worth your while. I'll pay you half a mil to just kidnap the bitch and get her to the holding place. I will handle the rest after that." He said.

Whoever he was trying to take out must have been

fucking up his money big time for him to want to pay half a mil just for me to snatch someone up. I would be a fool not to take this job.

"I'll do it, but I'm gonna do it on my terms. I want half up front, and the other half when the job is finished. I will text you my account information, and you can transfer the money there. After I get the money, hit me with a text and some background info on the person." I told him.

"Ight" he said.

I got up from the table and left. There was nothing else for me to talk to him about. Plus, I didn't like getting into details about my jobs in public places.

Jay

I was busy trying to make sure that everything was set up for the next couple of weeks, when I got a phone call, letting me know that things went well in the meeting, and that everything would be handled with in a month or so. I was glad this whole thing was going to be over, because it was starting to get on my nerves. Nick had been acting funny towards me, like I was the enemy. I tried to talk to Trey about it, but he just kept saying that Nick is going through a lot of shit right now. I didn't really care for all of that bullshit, cause at the end of the day, there was money to be made. There was a knock at my door, which pulled me out of my thoughts.

"Jay, wassup," Pops said, coming into my bedroom.

"Nothing, just making sure that everything is everything." I said.

"Do you think they are catching on?" He asked.

"Nah, I don't think so. Nick is acting funny, but he won't act on anything, which gives us a little more time." I told him.

"Ight, cause we got to end this shit and fast. I'm ready

to go lay up on a beach somewhere." he said.

I moved closer to him. Me and Pops always had this sexual tension between us. The only reason we never acted on it was because the timing was never right. But the timing couldn't have been better right now. I walked up to him and unbuttoned my shirt. I slipped it off and just stood in front of him.

"Jay, what are you doing." he asked me.

"I know you want me, you always wanted me." I told him.

I picked his hands up and placed them on my breasts. I leaned forward and kissed him. At first, he didn't react, but after a while his hands started to roam my body, and he kissed me back. After that, it got hot and heavy. We was so into it, that we never even herd the bedroom door open.

"Yo, what they fuck?" I heard Trey say.

I forgot that I had asked him to come over here, so that I could discuss him taking over the family business.

"Trey, it's not what it looks like." I tried to say.

"Jay, save it. That line never worked, and it never will work." He said, walking out of the room.

Me and Pops rushed to put our clothes on to catch up with Trey before he left the house, but by the time we got downstairs, he was gone.

"Do you think he was mad, or he was just surprised?" I asked Pops.

"He will be ight. But I gotta get going. I'll hit you later." He said, kissing me on my cheek.

I watched him walk out the door, and I got a little bit aggravated. I couldn't wait until this shit was over, so that I could go back to my regular life.

Trey

"Babe, what happened" Diamond asked.

95

I had went in to talk to Jay real quick cause she called me over. Diamond told me that she didn't wanna come in, and that she would wait in the car.

"Nothing, I just saw some crazy shit." I said, starting up the car.

"Well, whatever you saw, don't let it stress you too much cause tomorrow is a big day for us."

"Yea, I know. I don't know why we have to have a baby shower when we already got everything that we need."

"Because, we are going to celebrate our new addition to the family with our family." She said.

Only females wanted that extra shit. I just wanted a healthy baby. I really wasn't up for the whole partying thing. But my baby wanted it, so I gave her want she wanted. We decided to go to Party City to get the decorations for the party. Diamond said that Ny was cooking, so all we had to do was set everything up, and I was cool with that.

"I'm in the mood for some curry goat." Diamond said.

"I can go for some, too. Let's go to Golden Crust before we go home."

"That's cool with me." she said.

We stopped at Golden Crust on our way home. When we got in the house, I got a text from Jay, saying that some shit just went down, and that I needed to get to the trap out in Bedstuy ASAP. I tried calling Nick, but his shit was going straight to voice mail. I sent him a quick text, letting him know what happened and that I would handle it.

"Diamond, I got to go." I told her.

"Trey, come on, I thought we was going to spend the rest of the night together."

"Ma, you know I want to, but this is important. I'll be back as soon as I'm done, I promise. I kissed her on her forehead and kissed her stomach.

"I love you, Trey" she said.

"I love you, too," I told her, walking out the door.

Chapter 12

Nick

"Nick, come on, you can't live in a hotel forever."
Honey said

"I'm not going to. When I'm ready to get my own place, then I will do so, but for now, I'm chilling" I told her.

Ever since Honey came back into town, we have been kicking it. Trey said that it was a bad idea, cause he knew that once me and Ny worked things out, we would be cool, and that Ny wouldn't like the fact that I was entertaining other bitches. But I told Trey that we were just friends, shit, I didn't even hit it.

"Whatever you say, Nick." she said, getting off the bed.

Trey's baby shower was tomorrow, and I didn't pick up a gift yet.

"Yo, come with me, I have to pick up a gift for the baby shower tomorrow." I told her

"Why would you wait until nine at night to go get a present? I swear, only men do this shit."

"Whatever, let's just go."

We got in the car and went to Babies R Us. I wanted to ask Bee if she wanted to come to the baby shower with me, but it seemed like it was too soon for all of that to happen. We walked into the store, and I just started throwing everything into the cart. It was for my God child, so I didn't mind going all out.

"Boy, do you wanna slow down? You're not even looking at what your buying." Bee said, laughing.

"It doesn't matter, my God daughter deserves it all" I told her.

We started walking into the next aisle when I heard her voice.

"I don't know why I always wait until last minute to do stuff." She said, giggling.

I looked up, and there was Nylah, but she wasn't alone. She was with that nigga that I told her to stay away from.

"Nylah, so this is what we doing now? I thought I told you I better not catch the two of y'all together." I said.

"Nick, who is your little friend?" She said, with a smirk on her face.

"Don't worry about who the fuck she is. What are doing with this nigga?" I asked her again.

"Nick, it is none of your business who I am around, cause you're the one that just up and left after you fucked me." She said.

"You know what, you're right, it's none of my concern. But Play Boy, your days are numbered." I told him and then walked away.

I was so beyond pissed, that I just left the cart full of stuff and walked out. Nylah thought this shit was a game. I wasn't doing nothing wrong but chilling with a friend, but her, I knew what she was doing was personal. It was personal because I told her to stay away from that nigga.

"So, that must have been your girlfriend." Honey said.

I forgot she was even in the car I was so pissed off.

"Yea, that's her, but look I'm bout to drop you off, ight."

"That's fine," she said.

This is why I could fuck with her, cause she was just laid back and wasn't clingy. I dropped her off and told her that I would catch up with her later. I went straight over to Ny's house cause this shit was ending tonight.

Nylah

Nick had a lot of fucking nerve to be mad at me when he was out with some bitch. It didn't click until that bitch left, but that was the same bitch that was riding his dick in that video. I couldn't believe he would do some shit like that to me. He swore up and down that he didn't fuck no bitch that night, and he was walking around with her like shit was all peachy keen.

"Are you okay?" Demetri asked me.

"Yea, I'm ight, let's go pay for this stuff, so I can go home."

"Ight, ma"

Demetri was really a cool guy. We had been texting and just kicking it since I gave him my number earlier this week. He was just fun to be around, and he kept my mind off of Nick.

"So, what are you going to do when you finish school" He asked as we were driving back to my house.

"I wanna open my own business. I'm not sure exactly what I wanna own. I just know that I want to put my degree to use." I told him.

"Ambitious I see. I like that."

"Yea, well, I can't live off a nigga. I have to get my own."

"That's what I like to hear. We need more women like you around."

"Oh shut up, there are a lot of women with the same values that I have. You just have to look."

"I don't need to look, ma, cause the one I want is right here." he said.

I blushed cause I hadn't gotten this much attention in a while. Even though I wasn't ready to start dating again, I did enjoy the male attention. We continued talking. When we got to my house, he helped me bring the bags upstairs. As soon as I unlocked the door, I saw Nick sitting in the living room. Oh shit, I thought to myself, I knew that some shit was going to start.

"Where do you want the bags?" Demetri asked, walking in the door.

I couldn't answer cause my eyes were stuck on Nick. The vein that was on the side of his forehead was throbbing.

"My nigga, just drop the bags and get the fuck out" Nick said.

"Nylah, where do you want these bags?" Demetri said.

I knew I had to get Demetri out of there before Nick got his ass up.

"Nick, just drop them right there and leave." I said.

"Damn, Ny, why you have to violate and call that nigga by my name?" Nick said, laughing.

I didn't even know that I called him Nick. Shit, this was getting out of control.

"Nick, just shut up. Demetri, do you mind leaving, so I can handle this situation?" I asked him.

"Yea, ma, no problem, call me when you're done handling your little issue." He said.

"My nigga, who you calling a little issue?" Nick said, getting up and walking towards him.

"You heard what I said. If you knew how to handle your business, I wouldn't be in the picture."

Aww shit, this was getting too out of hand. Next thing I knew, Nick had his gun out pointed at Demetri.

"I suggest you get the fuck out of here before I blow your brains out." Nick said.

"My nigga, you're not the only one with them thangs." Demetri said, pulling out his gun, too.

I rushed to get in between the both of them.

"Nick, stop it, please." I said.

"Ny, you really gonna tell me to stop when this nigga got a gun pointed at me?"

"Demetri, just walk away, please."

Demetri lowered his gun and started backing out of the door.

"This ain't over, but this will be the last time you pull out a gun on me thought." He said, turning around and leaving.

Pow! I ducked as Nick shot at Demetri.

"That was just a warning. Next time, I won't miss." Nick said, slamming the door.

I got off of the floor and started to go upstairs before Nick stopped me.

"Where do you think you're going?" He asked me as he walked back to the couch.

"I'm going upstairs to take a shower. I have a long day ahead of me tomorrow."

"No, your gonna bring your ass over here, and we are going to talk this out."

"What is there to talk about? You obviously moved the fuck on!" I yelled at him.

"I was out with a friend, getting a gift for the baby shower tomorrow."

"Oh, so, that's what we call bitches we fucking now, friends."

"I didn't fuck her. What are you talking about?"

"Nick, don't play stupid with me. That's the bitch that was on the video with you."

"We back to that shit now. I'm not sure what you watched, but that wasn't me on no video fucking anyone."

"Yea, whatever, Nick, I know what I saw."

"Fuck that video! Why did you have this nigga in my house, shit, why were you even walking with this nigga?"

"Nick, I am grown. I can do whatever I want, when I want. How is this your house, if you don't even fucking live here? I can't even remember the last time your ass was here."

"Ny, I'm not going to tell you this again. If I see you with him; you are dead. That nigga already got a death sentence." He said.

I started crying, not because he said he was going to kill me, or because he said Demetri had a death sentence. I was just tired of this whole shit. I was going through drama after drama, and I was tired of it. This was all Elle's fault. I had been looking for that bitch, but it seemed like she fell off the face of the earth.

"Ny, come here, stop crying," Nick said.

I walked over to him and just laid my head on his chest. I was over the fighting and the not being together phase of this bullshit. I wasn't sure what needed to be done for us to fix things, but I was down to do about anything.

"Nick, I can't go through this shit, it's either we are going to be together, or we're not. This back and forth thing is way too stressful."

"Just answer me one question. Did you fuck him?"

I couldn't believe his dumb ass just asked me that question.

"No, I didn't fuck him. And if I did, you wouldn't try to work things out with me? You know what Nick, get the fuck out." I pushed him off of me, and I stormed upstairs.

What type of female did he think I was for me to just up and fuck the next nigga? Like, come on, I thought he knew me better than that, but I guess not.

Demetri

This nigga must have thought that shit was a game. If it wasn't for Ny, he would have splattered all over her apartment. My patience was really starting to wear thin with him. Me and Ny have been kicking it since I got her number. It has been cool, I know that her bitch ass boyfriend is the reason that she doesn't want to move on. But it was ight, cause I was gonna take care of everything. I was driving to the bar, so that I could meet up with Javon about this job. He needed to make sure that everything went the way that he wanted it to. I didn't really give a fuck about how he wanted shit done. I was gonna get it done the way I felt it was necessary. I walked in and saw him sitting in the back. I ordered a rum with coke and went and sat down.

"Did you get your funds?" He asked me.

"Yea, everything was straight."

"Ight, so look, the chick's name is Nylah. Nylah Royce Taylor. She is a part of the Royce family. I need her out of the picture."

I couldn't believe this shit. When he said the name, I figured it was my Nylah, but when he slid the picture in front of me, it confirmed everything.

"Why do you need her out of the way? Does she help with the empire?"

"Nah. From what I know, she just goes to school. Her boyfriend, brother, and mother run the empire. But if she turns up missing, they will be tearing this city up looking for her, which leaves the business aspect open for the taking."

What he said made sense, but damn, did it have to be Nylah though? I couldn't decline the job after I took the money, plus, I didn't really have an excuse as to why I couldn't do the job anyway. He gave me a little bit of back history on Nylah. I was half listening cause I wasn't interested anymore, but I knew that a job was a job, and I had to put my personal feelings to the side.

Elle

Guess who was back in town? I came back because it was time for me to put the final part of my plan together. I was going to hit Ny where it hurt. Then, I was gonna leave Brooklyn all together. Brooklyn just wasn't the place for me anymore. I felt like I outgrew the place. Growing up in Brooklyn is not the easiest thing. You got the jealous bitches that wanna fight just to fight, and then you had the sneaky ones that just wanted to see you fall. I wanted something more out of life than all of this. That's why once I was done, I was leaving for good. Bee called me and told me that she was on her way over. I was glad that I gave Bee a chance. She was what I wanted from Ny but could never get. She showed me the type of love and passion that I tried to show Nylah. There was a knock at my door, and when I opened it, Bee was standing there with a big smile on her face.

"Why you so happy?" I asked her while I watched her walk in my house.

She didn't have a lot of ass, but she had a good enough amount.

"I have the perfect idea. Okay, you know how I been telling you that I have been feeling sick lately. Well, I took a pregnancy test, and guess what's cooking in this oven!" She said, a little too happy for my liking.

"Wait, how the fuck did you get pregnant?" I asked her.

"Well, the drug I gave him was GHB, and even though he passed out, his dick didn't."

"You fucked him raw? That wasn't part of the plan, Bee."

"I know it wasn't, but this can help us even more. Nylah will never be with him after knowing that he got another chick pregnant. Plus, we will be straight cause he will be paying for this kid for the next eighteen years."

I couldn't believe this shit.

"Well, look at you, you figured this whole shit out didn't you? But tell me, what are you going to do if he finds out that he was raped?"

"Whatever, I'm not worried about that, cause who is ever going to believe that? But to add icing to the cake, there is a baby shower tomorrow, and I think that will the perfect time to tell everyone the good news."

"I don't think you should tell him so soon. Wait a while. At least until you start showing, so that it will really fuck with them." I told her.

I was gonna let her handle this part of the plan, but

telling Nick tomorrow would be a little too soon.

"Okay, I'll wait, but I don't wanna wait too long." she told me.

"Don't worry, you won't, you just have to wait long enough, so he can't force you to get an abortion." I told her giving her a kiss.

She told me not to worry, and that she would handle everything. I was tired of talking about this, so I told her to come get in the shower with me. I needed to release some stress, and Bee was just the person to help me do that.

<u>Chapter 13</u>

Nylah

I was up early, trying to get all this cooking done for the baby shower. I didn't get much sleep last night because of everything that went on with Nick. I was trying to take a pan out of the oven when my phone rang.

"Hello," I said, annoyed.

"Eww, why you answering the phone like that?" Diamond asked, laughing.

"Cause I am up early as hell cooking for your baby shower, and I didn't get any sleep last night." I told her.

"Why didn't you sleep, and if you need help, I'll come over there to help you."

"You know you're pregnant ass isn't going anywhere. I didn't get any sleep cause Nick's ass came over here last night."

"Oh shit, y'all made up. It's about time. I was tired of y'all asses."

"No, bitch, we didn't make up. I was in Babies R Us last night with Demetri, trying to find your gift, when we ran into him and some bitch. We exchanged words, and then when I got back to the house, this nigga was in the living room."

"Damn, did y'all at least talk shit through?"

"Nah, we yelled, and then when we seemed to be getting back on track, this nigga asked me did I fuck Demetri."

"Why would he ask some shit like that?"

"That's the same shit I asked him. Like, I thought he knew me better than that. After he said that shit, I just went upstairs and started crying."

"That's crazy. Where is he at now?"

"Upstairs, in the guest bedroom, sleeping. This is

probably all my fault though. If I never made Elle feel some type of way, then Nick would have never seen that video, and we would probably be planning our wedding right now."

"You can't blame yourself for other people's actions. Elle wanted something from you that you couldn't give her, and instead of her accepting that, she felt as though she needed to get payback. But she will get hers sooner or later. I'm sure that once y'all get over this rough patch, y'all will get married, and your ring will be beautiful."

"My ring is already beautiful." I told her.

"What you mean?"

"The night of the shoot out when me and Nick were outside, he proposed to me. We didn't tell anyone because we knew that shit was about to get hot in the streets, so we decided to wait and tell everyone."

"Damn, Ny, just give it time, y'all will work everything out."

"I know we will, Diamond, and I want to, but it is all up to him. But I have to get back to cooking, so everything can be done on time. I'll call you when I get done, and I'm on my way."

"Okay, and Nylah, don't worry, everything will work itself out. Oh, and it's okay to not be so tough sometimes."

"Thanks, Diamond."

I hung up and let her words sink into my head. I took the baked macaroni and cheese out of the oven, and when I turned around, Nick was just standing there.

"Make some noise when you walk in the room." I told him.

I wasn't sure how long he was standing there, or how much he heard.

"Good morning to you, too. You look like you need some help." He said.

"I really do. I really haven't been there to help Diamond with the baby shower like I said I would, so I volunteered to cook everything."

"Just tell me what you need me to do, and I got you."

We spent the whole morning cooking and talking and enjoying each other's company. This was the first time in months that we spent this much time together without arguing. It reminded me of how we used to be. These are the times that I missed. I wished we could just go back to being how we used to be.

"Ny, you know I missed you, right." Nick said, as he started to clean up the kitchen.

We had finish cooking everything by noon, and now, all we had to do was get dressed and be on our way.

"I missed you, too, Nick."

"I want us back. Whatever happened these past couple of moments, let's just leave it in the past and move on."

"Nick, I don't know, you believe that I did some shit, and I believe that you did some shit. It just doesn't feel right."

"Come on, Ny, I believe when you say that the video was old. Now you saying that I slept with some chick. I have no idea what you're talking about."

"Not some chick, the bitch you was with yesterday."

"I never slept with Bee. We just kicked it from time to time." he said.

I wanted to believe him; the proof was in the pudding. But I was gonna just let it ride and try to make this work.

"Okay, Nick, I hear you, but we are gonna have to take this one step at a time. We just can't jump back into the happy home."

"Ny, I know that, and don't worry, I got this, ma." He told me and gave me a kiss.

I was glad that we were gonna work on things, but I wasn't going to get my hopes up just yet. I knew that I had to stop talking to Demetri if I wanted things to work. I also knew that I had to warn him about Nick, I wouldn't feel right about Nick killing him, because the blood would be on my hands.

We cleaned up the kitchen, got dressed and packed everything into Nick's truck. I was beyond tire, but I was going to push through it for my baby. I couldn't wait until my God daughter was born. Being around Diamond had me thinking about having kids, especially now, because my period was a month late. I was too scared to take a test, because Nick and I wasn't even on talking terms before. I knew I had to make a doctor's appointment and quick. I figured I would make an appointment in the upcoming week, and that once I found out, I would tell Nick, but for now, it will be just my little secret. We pulled up to the house, and there were pink streamers everywhere. Nick started bring the food in the house, while I grabbed the gifts.

"Y'all came together?" Trey asked, helping us carry the stuff in.

"Yea, I guess you could say that." I told him.

"Ny, don't play, ight," Nick said.

"Yes, Trey, me and that big baby over there came together." I said, laughing.

"It's about time y'all got it together. Now, let's go get this party started." He said.

I finished helping Diamond set everything up, and by the time we was done, the guests were coming in. Jay and Pops came together, some of the girls from school came and Diamond's mom came and some of the dudes that rolled with Nick and Trey came through. We was all having a good time, playing games, eating and listening to music. The guys were on one end, and us girls were on the other, having a conversation about love.

"I see that you and Nick are back together." My mom said.

"Yea, we're working on us. It's not gonna be walk in the park, but I'm willing to try." I told them.

"Girl, you better get your man. Nick is a good dude from what I can see." Diamond's mom said.

"He fine, too. If you don't want him, I'll snatch him

up." Tiffany, one of the girls from Diamond's class, said.
We all just looked at her like she was stupid.

"What, I'm just being honest." she said, laughing

"You better not play like that with Ny about her man.
She is known to pistol whip bitches over that dick." Diamond
said.

"You damn straight." I said, giving Diamond a high
five.

"Y'all are crazy as hell." my mother said.

"Ma, I'm pretty sure that you pistol whipped a couple
of bitches over my father." I said.

"You damn straight I did. I even bodied a couple of
them. Your father looked just like Omar Epps, and bitches
came after him by the flock."

"See, you just as crazy as I am. Shit, that's probably
where I get it from." I said, laughing.

We continued to laugh and joke and share stories
about our relationships in the past. I was really enjoying
myself, it was nice to go through a day without any drama, or
at least I thought there wasn't any drama.

Trey

"You about to be a dad, you ready for that?" Big
asked me.

"Honestly, it's not something that you can be ready
for. The most you can do is get your mind right and be the
best father that you can be." I said.

"I hear that," Nick said.

"So, wassup with you and Ny?" I asked him.

"Nothing really, I went over there last night after I
seen her with dude. We just trying to work on shit. But I
think she pregnant; she getting thicker."

"Y'all both about to be dads. Damn, we gotta stop
hanging out with y'all, next thing we know, I'm have a chick

pregnant." Q said.

"You a fool, my nigga" Nick said.

"I'm just glad y'all are getting y'all shit together. I was tired of having to see my sister walking around looking sad and shit."

"Y'all young niggas let y'all problems sit and linger for too long," Pops said.

"What you mean?" Big asked.

"Instead of fixing the problem right when it happened, y'all wanna go months without talking to your lady, and then wanna come back and try to work things out. If y'all would fix the shit as soon as it happened, y'all wouldn't have to worry about other niggas moving in on your territory, and shit like that." He said, looking at Nick.

"I hear you, Pops," Nick said.

I felt like Pops was trying to hint at something. It could have been him wanting to talk to about what I saw that day when I came to Jay's house, but I didn't wanna talk about it cause I really didn't care. They were both grown, and what they did was there business. I had an announcement that I wanted to make. I was ready to settle down and leave this life alone. I was about to be a father to a baby girl, and I knew that I couldn't keep ripping and running the streets the way that I used to. I walked up to the DJ and asked if I could get everyone's attention.

"First off, I would like to thank everyone for coming out today and showing me and my girls love. Diamond, you know I love you, ma. You also know I am not all that good with words. You know I'm gonna be here for you and my daughter, regardless. This same year, I had I gained a sister and a mother, and I am grateful to have both of you in my life. I have all these incredible women in my life that I know my daughter will grow up knowing her worth. Diamond, you are it for me, ma, there is no other woman that could make me do what I am about to do."

I went in my pocket and pulled out the six carat

engagement ring that I had for Diamond. When I opened the box, all the females in the room gasped.

"Diamond, would do me the honors of being my wife?"

She got up and walked towards me shaking her head yes and crying. Before I could get her into my arms, shots rang out. Two dudes dressed in all black, walked in with guns drawn,they started shooting causing everyone to try and find cover. Diamond leaped into my arms as I tried to shelter her from the bullets. I seen Nick, Big, Q, and Pops firing back. My main focus was making sure that Diamond was okay. After the gun fire stopped, I called Diamond's name, but she wasn't responding. I saw blood leaking. I turned Diamond over and saw that she had been shot.

"Help!" I yelled.

Pops was the first one to make it over to me.

"What happened? Is everything alright?"

"No! we have to get Diamond to the hospital! She's been shot!"

Me and Pops carried her over to the car. I sat in the back while her head rested on my lap. I had no time to explain to anyone what was going on. I had to get Diamond to the hospital before I lost the baby, or even worse, before I lost Diamond.

"Drive faster, Pops," I yelled from the back seat.

"Trey," I heard Diamond say, barely above a whisper.

"Shhhh, don't speak, bae, we on the way to the hospital now, just hold on a little longer."

"I love you, Trey."

"I love you, too, Baby."

I didn't know what I was going to do if I lost either one of my girls. We pulled up to Brooklyn hospital and Pops jumped out.

"We have a pregnant woman who has been shot."

Nurses came rushing out, taking Diamond inside. I followed them, but they said I couldn't go in the back. I was beyond pissed off. I swore on anything I loved that if something happened to my daughter or Diamond, whoever did this was going to have hell to pay.

Nick

Something wasn't right, I could feel it. Both the niggas that were shooting were dead. I had went out to the front to make sure that no one else was coming. And when I got there, I saw Jay talking to someone dressed in all black. I watched them talk before the guy got back in the car and sped off. I walked back into the back before she could see me. I put what I just saw in the back of my mind, so that I could go find Ny. When I walked back downstairs, I saw Trey and Pops carrying Diamond out to the car. I knew I had to find Ny and get to the hospital as soon as possible. When I found her, she was making sure that everyone was okay.

"Ny, come on, we have to go," I told her.

"Have to go where, and where is Diamond and Trey? Are they okay?"

"That's why we have to go, Diamond has been shot."

"Let's go now, Nick," she said.

"Where y'all going?" Jay asked.

"We'll be back," I told her.

I didn't want her to know too much of anything, because after what I saw, I didn't trust her. We got to the hospital in ten minutes flat. We went to the emergency room to see if we could find Trey.

"Did they say anything yet?" I asked Trey.

"Nah," he said.

I could tell that he was going through it, cause he wouldn't pick his head up. I knew that whoever did this, was gonna pay. Ny was sitting off into the corner by herself. I was worried about her, she wasn't crying or anything. She just had this look in her eye. We all just sat there waiting for the doctor to come out and tell us something. It seemed like the longer the doctor took, the madder we all got. Me and Ny rushed out so fast that we didn't even tell Diamond's mom.

"Ny, call Diamond's mom and tell her to come to the hospital."

"I already called her, she is on her way now."

"Family of Diamond Mitchell," the doctor said.

"I'm her husband," Trey said.

We gathered around to hear what the doctor had to say.

"The young lady was shot three times. Two of the bullets went up and hit her spine, and the other one went through her neck. We was not able to save her, but we did perform an emergency C-section. They baby wasn't due for another two weeks, so she is under weight. We want to keep her here to monitor her, and to make sure that she gains the weight of a full term baby."

"Thank you." Trey said and walked out of the hospital.

"When can we see the baby?" Ny asked he doctor.

"Y'all can go back there now to see the baby." The doctor said and walked off.

As soon as the doctor left, Diamond's mother came in. We explained to her what happened, and she broke down crying. Me and Pops tried to console her, but it seemed like nothing was working. I didn't like to deal with death, and I didn't really know how.

"Ms. M, come on, so we can go see the baby." Ny said.

She and Diamond's mom went into the back. While they were back there, I took the chance to talk to Pops about Jay.

"Yo, I seen Jay talking to one of them niggas. I guess he was the driver."

"Nah, you bugging."

"I'm dead ass, Pops. After we handled the two, I went

to the front to see if there were anymore, and when I got to the door, I seen Jay talking to a nigga in all black."

"I'ma talk to her and see what that was about. But don't worry about it, just make sure your there for both Trey and Ny." Pops said before he left.

Something was up cause Pops acted like he couldn't look me in the eye, which was strange, because Pops always looked us eye to eye. I had to put Trey on, cause some shit was about to go down, and we had to be prepared.

Chapter 14

Demetri

I have been trying to get in contact with Nylah for about two weeks now. But she was ducking a nigga. She wasn't answering my calls or my texts. I have been putting the job off for as long as I could, but this Javon nigga was starting to get on my fucking nerves. He said that I needed to move now, while these niggas were off their square. I wanted to give Nylah the heads up. I decided to call her one last time.

"What do you want?" She said with an attitude as soon as she picked up.

"Ma, calm down with all that attitude, shit." I told her.

"Nigga, I haven't been answering your calls or your texts, so I figured that you would get the hint already. Me and Nick are back together, I was just using you as someone to keep me company until we got our shit together."

"Ight, ma, say no more." I hung up.

Fuck her, I was just something to do, ight. I called Javon and told him that the job will be done this week and to have my money ready. I liked Nylah, but she wanted to act like she didn't enjoy the time we spent together, and I was just her toy, and she could throw me away when she wanted to. I didn't play those types of games, the least she could have done was call me and let me know what wassup, like a real woman would. But I would get the last laugh, cause I wasn't the nigga to play with.

Nylah

I felt bad for how I treated Demetri, but I was going

through a lot of stress right now. I figured once everything died down, I would call him and apologize, but for now, it is what it is. No one has herd from Trey in the last two weeks. He wasn't answering nobody's phone calls or texts. The hospital said that they saw him a couple of times, when he visited the baby, but that was it. We were all worried about him, especially with Diamond's funereal being tomorrow. Nick had been acting strange, too, like he was keeping something from me. On top of that, Diamond's mom wasn't doing so good. I haven't talked to my own mother since the day the shooting happened. She told me that she had to go back to Miami because some shit came up, I found that shit strange, too. It was like, when we needed each other the most, no one was really around. I made all the funeral arrangements, because Diamonds mom said she wasn't up for it. I went to go see the baby twice a day, and on top of that, I found out that I was two months pregnant. I must have gotten pregnant the day Nick fucked me and then left me. I haven't told Nick, cause I didn't want to add any more stress to his plate.

"What you over there thinking about?" Nick asked, walking into the kitchen.

He scared the shit out of me. I hated that when he walked around the house, he never made any noise.

"Nothing, just thinking about everything that has been going on," I told him, giving him a kiss before sitting on the counter.

"Ma, don't stress yourself, everything is going to be fine, I got this."

"Nick, you can't handle everything by yourself, let me help you."

"Ma, you are helping me by staying out of harm's way. If something was to happen to you, I wouldn't know what I would do."

"I know. Have you talked to Trey?"

"Yea, he hit him up today, talking about he wants to

meet up with me."

"Good, at least someone has heard from him. He really shouldn't be alone right now. We all need each other."

"Ma, don't worry. Trey just needed sometime to himself, so he can get his mind right. He just lost the love of his life after proposing to her, and then on top that, his daughter is in the hospital. It was a lot for him to handle. He just needed a break."

"I know, but when you see him, tell him I miss him, and that I love him."

"I will. But do you have something to tell me?" He asked me, looking at me funny.

I didn't know if he knew that I was pregnant or not, so I decided to keep that little bit of information to myself.

"No, why do you ask?" I asked, avoiding eye contact.

"Ma, I know you're lying, but I'ma let you rock. Can you cook me something to eat before I go meet up with Trey? A nigga is hungry."

"Yea, I got you. What you want to eat?"

"It doesn't matter, I just need to eat. I'ma go get in the shower, call me when the food is done." He said walking up stairs.

I got off the counter and started to cook him something to eat. It was the afternoon, so I decided to make him chicken and fries. When I was finished, I called Nick down stairs. When he came down, I just stared at him. He was so handsome. He wasn't all dressed up, he kept it simple with a pair of sweats, a black t-shirt and the bred 11's.

"What you looking at me like that for?" He asked, taking a fry off his plate.

"No reason just looking."

"Yea, whatever, but what you doing today?"

"Nothing, everything is set for funeral. I visited the baby earlier this morning. The doctor said that she is doing great and should be home in no time."

"So, come ride with me to go see Trey."

"Are you sure that's a good idea? I mean, he did say that he wanted to talk to you." I said unsure if I should go or not.

I didn't know what Trey wanted to talk to Nick about, but I didn't wanna get in the way or anything.

"You're his sister. I'm sure its fine, now go upstairs and get dressed, cause as soon as I'm done, we leaving."

I ran up the stairs and threw on some sweats and a t shirt. I put on my running sneakers and threw my curly hair in a bun. When I came back downstairs, Nick was finished and ready to go. I just shook my head at him cause the way he ate was crazy. I was up stairs for twenty minutes, and he ate his food that fast.

"You have an appetite like a horse with the way that you eat." I told him as we walked out of the door.

He just laughed and got in the car. I was happy that we were going to see Trey cause I really missed him, and with Diamond gone, him, Nick, my mother, and the baby was really all the family I had left.

Trey

I know that I had people worried about me for the last two weeks, but I just needed time to get my head straight. I couldn't believe that she was gone. Every time I went to go see my daughter, I saw Diamond's face. My daughter meant the world to me. She was my ray of sun shine in my dark world. I have been putting my ear to street to find out who did this Diamond, and I found out that it was Javon. When I told Jay, she said she would handle it, but the last I heard, she up and left to Miami. What kind of shit was that? The mother of your grandchild was dead, and you just up and leave when your family needs you? I was starting to believe that this whole family shit was a lie, cause for our name to mean so much, it damn sure wasn't helping us. I called Nick and told him that I wanted to talk to him because I felt like he was the only person I could trust. I wouldn't feel right until Javon was found and dead. I wanted to be the one to personally deliver him to his maker. I heard a knock on the door. When I looked out the peep hole, I saw Ny's little ass standing there with a big ass smile on her face.

"What are you doing here?" I asked her as I opened the door to let her in.

"Nick told me that he was coming to see you, and I wanted to come to check up on you. Don't tell me you didn't miss me." she said, taking off her jacket.

"Of course, I missed you, come give me a hug."

"Aye, aye, get off my girl, nigga." Nick said, walking into the room.

"Shut up, this is my sister. I can do what I want." I told him, giving him a hug.

I was genuinely glade to see the both of them.

"Y'all don't have to fight over little ole me, I have enough love to go around for the both of y'all." She said, causing us to laugh.

"But wassup though, what did you want to talk about?" Nick asked as he sat at the table.

Me and Ny followed him. I wasn't sure if I wanted Ny to hear what I was going to say. I didn't wanna get her involved in this shit. I already lost Diamond. I didn't want to lose my sister, too.

"I can already see what you are thinking. I'm letting you know now, Diamond was my girl, and I want to help y'all get revenge. I know both of y'all are worried about something happening to me, but I can handle myself." Ny said.

I just looked at Nick, and he shrugged his shoulders. He knew, just like I did, that it didn't matter if we told Ny no, she was still going to do what she wanted to do.

"Ight so look, I asked Nick here cause right now he is the only nigga I trust. Well, I trust you too Ny, but I didn't expect you to be here. Anyway, I have been doing some looking, and I found out that Javon was behind the shoot, which is something that we already knew. But what we didn't know is that they still have somebody on the inside telling them shit."

"How you find that out?" Nick asked.

"One of my homies on 125th said that a nigga that rolled with the Maxwell family was talking about how they bout to take over, and how they got niggas on the inside and that it will make their come up easier."

"I know who it is." Nick said.

Me and Ny just looked at him. I could tell that there was something wrong, because Nick was hesitant about saying who it was.

"Well, who is it?" Ny asked.

"It's Jay," Nick said.

"What you mean it's my mother? Why would she help them?"

"I'm not sure why she would do that, but I know the day of the shooting I went to the front to see if there were any more niggas, and I saw her talking to a nigga that was dressed in all black."

"Okay, but that could have been anybody." Ny said.

I could tell that she was letting her emotions cloud her better judgment.

"Come on, Ny, if niggas is shooting, why would she be out in the front just having a conversation with someone?" I said, trying to get her to realize the truth.

"Okay, but what else y'all got on her?"

"I'm not gonna lie, I was thinking that something was up with her, too. Cause how she supposed to be the head of the Royce family, but she can't find one fucking guy? On top of that, where is she right now?" I asked.

"She went to Miami to handle business," Ny said.

"Correct me if I'm wrong, she claims that she stayed away because she didn't want nothing to happen to her family. But ever since she came back, there has been nothing but chaos, and she hasn't done not a damn thing about it."

I was on the verge of yelling and losing my cool. I didn't care if she was supposed to be my mother or not, she was acting shady.

"True," Ny said.

I could tell that she was hurt by the accusation that me and Nick put on Jay. But the facts were the facts.

"So, what's your plan?" Ny asked.

"The same dude that told me that we had a leak on our squad knows where the dude that was running his mouth hangs out at. After the funereal tomorrow, I wanted to snatch his ass and see what he got to say."

"Ight, but I'ma call big and Q, so that they can ride with us., cause we don't wanna be walking into no traps. We got to play this shit carefully." Nick said.

"I can do it." Ny volunteered.

"You can do what?" Me and Nick asked at the same time.

"I can go over there, flirt a little, and then take him back to the spot where y'all are going to be waiting at." she said.

It was an ight plan, but I still didn't want her to get in the middle of this shit.

"Nah, Ny I'm not letting you do that shit." Nick said.

"Come on, I'm part of this family, too, and just like y'all, I'm hurting from Diamond's death. You acting like I don't know how to use a gun or set someone up before."

I guess she was referring to when she set up Jacob. She had a point. Ny did know how to handle herself, and it would make shit easier, but it was really up to Nick.

"Ok, you can do it, but you will be followed at all times just in case something goes wrong." Nick said.

"Fine," Ny said.

She seemed a little too happy about the whole thing, but I wasn't gonna put her on front street. We called Big and

Q and told them to roll through. Once they got there, we went over the plan with them, too. We figured after the burial we could go do what we got to do, and make back to the house by the time everyone else got there. Visiting hours were almost over, and I wanted to go see my baby. So, we all got in our cars and drove up to the hospital. The doctor told me that I needed to name my daughter and sign the birth certificate. At first, I didn't know what to name her. I know that me and Diamond agreed on naming her Arielle, but with Diamond gone, I wanted our daughter to be a remembrance of her. So, I decided on Arielle Diamond Royce. My daughter was my world, and I would do any and everything to make sure that she was okay and safe.

Chapter 15

Brielle

    I had heard what happened to Diamond, and I honestly felt bad. No child should have to grow up without a mother. I wanted to attend the funereal but didn't know how everyone would react to me being there. Bee has been getting on my nerves about contacting Nick and telling him that she was pregnant. I knew that right now would have been the perfect time to drop the bomb, but even I wasn't that evil.

    I figured I would go to the funeral anyway just to pay my respects.

    "Where are you going? It's only eight in the morning." Bee said, rolling over.

    "I'm gonna go to the funereal to pay respects." I told her.

    "Why, you didn't even like her." she said.

    I was stuck because she did have a point. I didn't like Diamond, but I still wanted to go, so that was exactly what I was going to do.

    "So what, we still had some fun times together."

    "Well if you're going, than so am I." She said, getting up out of the bed.

    "What are you going for?"

    "I'm going to make sure you don't get into no shit. Now, let's go get in the shower, we don't want to be late."

    I just stared at her like she had fifteen heads. I wasn't in the mood to argue with her, so I jumped in the shower, too. We both choose to wear black form fitting dresses with black sling backs. When we pulled up to the church, everybody who was anybody was there. I pulled my shades down over my face because I didn't wanna be seen. We watched as Ny, Nick, Trey, and I guessed to be Diamond's mom walked in and sat in the front row. It really was a beautiful service.

After it was over, I was ready to go. I figured that I didn't need to stay for the burial because that was a bit much.

"You ready to go, Bee?"

"You're not staying for the burial?"

"No, why would I? That is for close family and friends, and I am not either one of those."

"Okay, well just let me go say hi to Nick first."

"I hope you know you are signing your own death certificate."

"Wasn't you the one that wanted to get back at Nylah for all the shit that she has put you through?" she asked me.

It was true, I wanted to get back at Nylah, but it all didn't seem worth it now. I felt like she had been through enough already without me adding anymore drama.

"That is what I thought. Just because you had a change of heart doesn't mean that I did. She took you away from me, and now she has to pay for not treating you the right way." Bee said and started walking in the direction of Nick.

I had created a monster. I wanted Nylah to feel my pain, but I never wanted it to go this far. There was a baby involved now, and it seemed like Bee didn't care.

Nick

"I'm sorry for your loss." I heard someone say behind me.

When I turned around, I saw Bee.

"Uh, thanks, but what are you doing here?" I asked her.

Nylah and Trey were talking to Diamond's mom, but they would be back soon, and I didn't wanna get caught talking to the same chick Nylah told me to stay away from.

"I've been looking for you. I have something to tell you."

"What could you possibly have to tell me?"

"I'm pregnant." she said.

"What are you telling me for? I never fucked you."

"You never fucked who?" Nylah asked, walking up behind me.

"Hi, you must be Nylah," Bee said, sticking her hand out for Ny to shake.

"I am, and who are you?" Nylah asked her.

"I'm the mother of his baby," Bee said, pointing at me.

"Honey, what are you doing here?" Trey asked, walking up to us.

"Honey? I thought your name was Bee." I said, confused.

"My name is Honey, but my friend gave me the nickname Bee since they like honey. Get it?" She said, laughing like this shit is funny.

"Wait, did you just say you are his baby's mother?" Ny said, pointing at me.

"Yes, I did, and Trey, I'm sorry for your loss."

"Trey, how do you know her?" I asked.

"I used to fuck her every now and again. How you know her?" He asked me.

"That day I went to the bar I was too drunk to drive, so she drove me to the motel." I said.

We was so caught up in trying to figure out who this bitch was, that we never noticed Ny taking off her shoes and earrings.

"Well, apparently you get around, so good luck finding you baby daddy." I told her.

"I already found him. You are my baby daddy. You don't remember me riding your dick in your car?"

Pow! As soon as she finished those words, Nylah punched her in her face. I grabbed Ny before she could do anymore damage because she was pregnant. She didn't know, that I knew, for some reason she was keeping it from me.

"Nick, get the fuck off of me! I told you that you fucked that bitch in your car. And she has the nerve to come up here disrespecting my best friend's funereal? She deserve this ass whooping."

I ignored everything she was saying. I put her ass in the car and put the child safety lock on. I told the driver to not let her out of the car and to take her home. I went back over to where Trey and Bee were to straighten this shit out.

"Look, I don't know who you think your baby father is, but I know it wasn't me. I never fucked you, and I never will. So, get your shit and leave. You wasn't welcomed here to begin with." I told her.

"Nigga, you and your bitch is gonna pay for this, mark my words." She said, walking away.

I didn't have time for this dumb shit, we had moves to make. After the burial, me and Trey went back to the house to go get Ny. I was calling and texting her the whole time, but she wasn't answering. I figured she was just mad about what happened and was trying to ignore me. When we got to the house, I called out to her, but nobody responded. We searched the whole house, but she wasn't there. I called her phone, and this time somebody answered.

"Nylah," I said in to the phone.

"No, this is not Nylah," some bitch said.

"Put Nylah on the phone."

"I can't do that right now. She is a little busy at the moment."

"Bitch, put Nylah on the fucking phone!"

"Is that how you talk to people when you want something?"

I didn't know who this was on the phone, but she was pissing me the fuck off.

"Look, can you just put Nylah on the phone?"

"See, was that so hard now?"

"Nick! Help me!" I heard Nylah say.

"Ny, where are you?"

127

"Don't worry about where she is. You need to worry about who she is with."

"If you hurt her, we are gonna have problems."

"It amazes me how you're on the losing side of this, but yet, you are still making threats."

I didn't know who this person was, but she was starting to piss me off with all this riddle shit.

"What do you want?"

"I want six million in cash."

"What makes you think that we got that type of money?" I asked her.

I wanted to know if she knew anything about us, or was she just winging it.

"I'm sure you got it. Plus, I sold you the shit that helped you get to where you are today, so I know y'all got it."

When she said that, I recognized her voice.

"Jay," I said.

"Yup, it's me," she said, laughing.

"How could you do this to your own daughter?"

"Oh, I'm not that Jay. Jazmine is dead."

"Then who the fuck are you?"

"I'm Jade, her twin sister." and with that she hung up.

"Yo, what happened?" Trey asked, coming into the living room.

"Ny has been kidnapped by Jay."

"Why would Jay kidnap her own daughter?"

"Because Jay wasn't who we thought she was."

"No, it couldn't be, I thought she was dead." Trey said.

"I guess no one really dies anymore."

To Be Continued.....

CPSIA information can be obtained at www.ICGtesting.com
Printed in the USA
LVOW08s0655250115

424084LV00044B/1788/P

9 781502 892492

Acknowledgments

First I would like to thank my supporters & the readers because without y'all I wouldn't be on my second book. Second I have to thank Jamal, if you wouldn't have got me mad that day then being a writer would just be something that I said I was gonna do but never following through with it. I love you papi.

To my brother Michael you are my hero, I have always looked up to you growing up. You are my best friend and I never want our relationship to change. Of course we fight what siblings don't, But no matter what I will always love you.

Shout out to Charmaine for giving me this opportunity. To the whole PPP family shout out to y'all for the support, I'm glad that I could be a part of this team.

To David Weaver I just want to say thank you for paving the way for other authors to do what they love. In the words of Tupac you are appreciated.

Iona my lil thug, we have only known each other for a couple of months but you are my bish. You have helped me when I have been stuck and when I wanna complain I know that you are there to listen and give me advice. I thank you for everything that you have done for me, and don't worry I know I owe you buffalo wild wings. I got you boo.

To everyone that has helped me to promote my book, that have read my book, and that gave me feedback I just want to say thank you so much cause it really means a lot.

To the readers if you ever want to contact me feel free to do so

Facebook: Kellz Kimberly

Instagram: rebelwitacause__

Once again thank you everyone.